Sanitarium Magazine
Issue no. 20

Thank you to all of our contributors, we couldn't have done it without you.

Contents

Dear Reader,

We welcome to you a slightly new looking Sanitarium. We would like to welcome our new cover artist Kevin Spencer to the team. His style we hope you agree is striking as well as beautiful.

Over the past 20 issues we have showcased just short of 200 stories, a great selection of dark verse, spent time with iconic and inspiring writers and long may it continue.

With your help and building on our successes we know we can do it. So please enjoy the latest issue and if you like what you read, please leave a review on Amazon. With each and every 'like' review and rating we can showcase more writers and artists.

Thank you again for your time and welcome to the Sanitarium.

Barry Skelhorn

Donor

Rayne KaaHedberg

Physician: Dr. Roundtree
8245-AVD12

"DOCTOR VERNON!"

Marie barged through the doors to the man's office, seeing him sit by his desk that was cluttered with all sorts of different files seemingly in no particular order, along with books spread open on various pages, and somewhere in the middle of all of it, a computer screen he had his eyes glued to. As soon as she entered the room he sprung up from his seat as if he had been caught watching blue film at work. His metal-rimmed glasses with aspheric lenses had slid down the bridge of his nose, and the man looked as if he hadn't slept in well over a day or two, dark lines displayed underneath his eyes. Marie slammed a bunch of paperwork onto the already filled desk so that some papers flew up in the air from the draft, only to descend to the floor. "You forged the paperwork on the man that came in here two weeks ago."

The Adam's apple bobbed up and down as the doctor swallowed, and then raked a hand through his hair that had begun to go grey by his temples.

"You don't understand, Marie…" he began, but his colleague was furious with him, and wouldn't listen to some petty excuses.

"You are a *doctor*! This is completely unacceptable, and you know that very well, Vernon. You can be sued for this– the whole hospital can get sued because of what you have done, do you realise that, what risk you put yourself through? All of us?"

"Don't you think I know?" he snapped back, covering his mouth with his fingers as soon as he had, as if he realised how sharp his response was. Starting to anxiously stroke his lips, Doctor Vernon then placed his hand to his side, the man's posture being a bit sloped, and looking as if it was in desperate need of support. "And getting sued is the least of my worries right now."

"What do you mean?"

Marie had to ask the question when they lived in a place, as well as a day and age where everyone was carefully trying to survive treading on a minefield where there were several of lawsuits lying around that could blow your entire future to smithereens. It could leave individuals as well as companies, no matter how wealthy they were, in complete ruin. When he then, especially as a doctor who had done something wrong, he would most definitely get sued for if anyone found out (which was only a matter of time), did not show any apparent fear over this it had her concerned over what those other worries that overshadowed it could be. The man sank down into his seat again, resting his fingers against his temple, the wrinkles by the corners of his eye temporarily being smoothed out by the skin being pulled back.

"I think he might have been infected."

Marie's jaw dropped. This was the man that had been working at the hospital for over twenty years, the one that had been around to tutor her when she was but an intern, and now he had done not only a crime that people with any sort of common knowledge knew was just that; a crime, but also a mistake that even the greenest sprout of an intern would had learnt before setting foot inside the hospital doors. He had gone against everything they stood for as doctors, and to that she didn't know what to say. The only reasonable explanation for his plain idiotic behaviour that was not only idiotic, but out of character would be if he would have a brain tumour that was pressuring at the wrong spots, causing him to think taking these decisions was a good idea. However, since he was an experienced doctor he probably would have picked up on the symptoms well before anyone else, and realised what it was to take the responsibility to stop working while getting treated for it, before something like this or worse happened.

"Are you out of your mind!? You didn't have him tested!?"

"Of course I did!" He sounded offended by her question. "What do you take me for?"

"I take you for a man who has clearly lost his mind."

"He was infected with something we haven't seen before," Doctor Vernon clarified, gesturing at what was currently covering his otherwise tidy desk, "something new."

Marie was silenced for a moment. Something new was what every doctor feared, a disease that they did not have a remedy for, something they were unable to cure.

"Vernon, what have you done…"

Taking off his glasses and putting them down, the doctor gestured for her to have a seat, and she slowly sank down to one of the chairs that were standing in front of the desk. Usually visitors used to sit in them when having a meeting with him about their treatment, a patient, or when the crucial moment of insurance came up as a question. Marie was afraid of what he was about to tell her, the situation apparently so much worse than she first expected, and it wasn't as if it was nothing to start with.

"The man that came in here had been in a motorcycle accident," he initiated. "The injury caused intracranial haemorrhage, and did not make it to the hospital. His other organs however were still in perfect shape…"

"Have you thought about what will happen if his family comes here and finds that you have harvested this man's organs?" she interrupted, unable to contain the frustration that was boiling inside of her like water in a kettle, and it would soon come to the point where she shrieked like the kettle would.

"That's what the forging of his papers were for. We made some marginal changes here, took some shortcuts there, so before you know it the man was a John Doe, and if no relatives showed up within three days he would fail to refuse donating his organs so they would be up for us to take. It would be seen as legal." She could hardly believe in what the man she had looked up to for so long was telling her when he had been the one who corrected her mistakes, and taught her the rules of the game. Now Vernon was the one breaking them without any shame in his tone when he said it, no remorse for the crime against the man in question's rights as a person. The respect she had put in him was slowly deteriorating, like a corroding copper pipe. "In this day and age there are so few that are willing to give up their organs for donation," the doctor continued, repeatedly pressing his finger down against the paper as to emphasise his point to make his crime excusable. "When an opportunity such as this comes up you can't afford to pass on it. His death was unfortunate, but it could save other people's lives!"

"That is a moral question," Marie replied, unable to look him in the eye, "and you have no right to decide over a person's body even after their death." As much as she would like to say that it was a good deed, and how the thought would have come to her mind at one point, Marie could not look past everything they had been taught during years of training, to be so disrespectful, and to put that person's family through such a thing. It was not their place to make such a choice. "What of his family?"

"The man was not from here. All I can say is that he wouldn't be missed."

There was a wave of disgust that swept through her when Doctor Vernon said that, along with a quivering chill that coursed down her spine. As if that would right his wrong, simply because he thought the man wouldn't be missed.

"What of the infection?" she proceeded instead, not wanting to stay on the prior subject for too long, and Marie still needed to know what the rest of the story entailed. Vernon laced his fingers together, absent-mindedly stroking his thumb over the skin of his hand in a soothing manner when he spoke of the rest.

"When the transplants were made everything was going perfectly. There were no complications from the patients other than the usual. The patients stayed up to ten days according to procedure so that we could monitor them, and make sure the patient's body did not reject the organ or there were any infections. Everything went perfectly, and one by one the patients who had been saved by this transplant got to return home."

Although it may sound very nice put like that, since the unknowing donator had some sort of infection it meant that the more people that had gotten any of his organs the bigger the risk of whatever this was increased. Not knowing if this would only affect the receiver of the organs, or if it was something that could spread it could in worst-case scenario lead to an epidemic.

"So, when did you discover that the so-called *John Doe* was infected with something you had never during your career as a doctor come across?"

"As you know the patients are required to return to the hospital for check-ups to see how they are faring, but before it was time to call them back, I got a call from the person who had gotten the heart transplant. He said he wasn't feeling very well, and that he was extremely tired, so I told him that it was very usual to feel that way, but if it got worse, he could come in here so that I could do an earlier check-up." The doctor began to bite at his nails as well as turning in his seat to gaze out the window, seemingly pale from thinking back to what had happened. If Marie wouldn't know better, she would say that he looked a bit green, almost as if he was battling with his intestines to not be sick right then and there, all over the important papers. "When he came in for his first check-up there seemed to be nothing wrong with him. The only thing that was a bit low was the amount of red blood cells in his system, but that was not so surprising, and could easily be solved by getting enough vitamin E, B2, and B12 through a well-adjusted diet. It would balance out in the end."

"Why do I get the feeling that it did not in fact balance out in the end?"

Doctor Vernon couldn't scowl at her scepticism, despite the fact that he would like to, but raised his shoulders when he held his hands out in the air, eyes widened in what she guessed was an attempt to defend himself.

"Everything he said was explainable! It had a logic explanation!" "What did he actually say?" she asked, deeply concerned as to where this was going.

"He was tired, felt "a bit groggy" and was constantly hungry." Now the man's brow furrowed, and his head shook. "He said no matter how much he ate he was always hungry."

"You ran some tests on him, right? Please tell me you ran tests on him."

"Of course I did!" A fist slammed down into the desk, even more papers falling down to the floor. "I am not an idiot; I have been in this line of business for over twenty years! I ran tests on him, and there were no significant abnormalities the first times."

"The first times?" Marie echoed.

"When he said he wasn't getting better," Vernon proceeded, now having gone back to being calm. "I asked him to come in, and he had…"

Doctor Vernon trailed off in the middle of his sentence, his eyes seeming to stare past the obstacle of the window, and beyond to a place unobtainable for Marie. This was no time for daydreaming, and so she cleared her throat to ask him with a stern tone, like a mother talking with her child, trying to get her said son or daughter to tell her exactly what happened that resulted in the plate being shattered against the floor: "He had what?"

"Bruises." The man let his hands hover over his arms, and chest. "All over his body. But this is very prone to happen whenever someone has an iron deficiency!" he was quick to add, holding up his index finger in the air. "It was clear to me then that he had anaemia, and needed to know how to treat this." His bottom lip began to quiver, a glimpse of something she interpreted as a mixture of fear and guilt detectable in his eyes. "But it was too late."

"What do you mean it was too late…?"

Being able to feel that he was soon to come to the part where the amount of how bad it could get reached its climax, Marie's hands tightened into fists in her lap, while Vernon rose from his chair, pacing back and forth behind his office chair with restless steps. "After I had tested him I told him to talk with his wife so that she would know he needed to return here for further observation. He said he would go home and wait for her to come back, so I sent the tests in to the lab in the meantime." The doctor stopped temporarily to look at Marie. "I ran tests on the others, too," he assured so that she would not get to ask him about it first, before beginning to pace back and forth again, now in a quicker pace. "Since I wanted to make sure there was nothing wrong with the organs, but only with this particular patient. All their tests came back normal, nothing to make note of; they were fine. But seeing now that I have the results it could be that since he got such a vital organ such as the heart it was able to spread faster, break down his immune system in an atrocious pace. I didn't know it was a virus then. Hadn't gotten the results, and everything had a reasonable explanation." The latter part seemed to be directed towards Vernon himself rather than to Marie. "Then when I get back I have two messages on my answering machine."

"Who were they from? What did they say?"

"The first one was from my patient. He said that I had to help him because there was something wrong with him. At first I could barely recognise his voice. It was much different from how it was usually, and it sounded… Deranged." His fingers flicked across his own throat, exposed when Doctor Vernon tipped his head back slightly, still keeping Marie in his gaze. "As if he had something stuck in his throat. And his breathing was abnormal. It was heavier than before, like if he was exhausted from having run a lap around his house. He said that he was hungry. That he couldn't take it any more…"

All these pauses were killing her as her colleague refused to get to the point, delaying it when as far as they knew time could be scarce if they needed to stop the breakout of an epidemic.

"And the other?" Marie inclined, her patience already being very short.

"It was from my brother Phillip, the police officer." The one that undoubtedly had helped him with covering up for the John Doe incident, Marie thought. "He said…"

"Yes?"

"He said that… that they had found my patient…" "And?"

"That he had… he had…"

When he had sunken into yet another pause, like an old man at the end of his days getting lost in nostalgia rather than a doctor that had been in practice for over two decades, and was very quick in thought despite for the fact that he wasn't one of the youngest at the hospital. To snap him out of it once and for all, Marie stood up, and slammed the palms of her hands into the desk, not thinking of the poor papers that were now covering their spots on the floor around them.

"Doctor Vernon!"

It seemed to have worked, as he tensed up, but then spat out what he had been sitting on for all that time.

"He had eaten his wife!"

Now it was her turn to lose hold on her vocabulary. She could barely take in what he had just told her to let her brain process it, but it was stuck in a stage where it couldn't figure out which format it was, like a computer trying to read a broken disk. Marie's mouth was agape, unable to produce any sound for the first minute. He couldn't be joking, Vernon would not joke of something like that, but he couldn't be serious either, so there she was trying to make what she had heard comply, like a child determined to make that piece of the jigsaw puzzle with the piece it did not in fact fit with by using force.

"He a… eaten…"

"He had eaten his wife," Doctor Vernon repeated, and now Marie could understand why he looked like he was going to be sick, since so did she. "He hadn't eaten all of her. Not digested all of it, but had taken… chunks out of her."

"Oh god," Marie gagged, bringing her right hand up to her mouth in order to prevent herself from being sick in his office. She couldn't wrap her mind around it. To go so far as cannibalism was something that did not simply happen overnight, but was often a matter of an idea, a seed planted at an early age such as the early adolescence, like you could see in those serial killers who consumed their victims, or for people who were put in extreme conditions such as long-lasting starvation. To hear how a seemingly normal person went from needing a heart to feeding off his wife was unreal, and it was almost so that she did not believe in it. If Marie hadn't been there to have the conversation with Doctor Vernon face to face, she most likely would not have believed. It was something far too extreme. Though, seeing as the situation the doctor had put himself, and the others, in they had to come up with a solution, do what they were entitled to do, which was to inform the authorities. This needed to be stopped, fast. "Why were you just sitting here until now?" Marie gritted her teeth, having an incredibly hard time to keep her panic quelled, her heart racing within her chest a clear giveaway for that.

"I was searching for anything that would match with the test results, anything at all as obscure as it could sound, no matter how old. I thought there had to be something you could do about it, something that would explain this, and then you barged in here with your paperwork."

"All right..." she muttered, brushing a strand of hair behind her ear. Think, they had to think rationally to eliminate this problem just like any other, and could not let fear take over them. Think, then act, but it was important that you did it in that specific order. In fact they had been trained to deal with crisis, although none of them Marie had been heard of had something to do with people starting to eat off each other when getting an infected organ with a mystery none of them had ever seen before. "Where was the man from? If you have his ethnicity there might be more information for us to find."

"He wasn't from here," Vernon replied, his gaze lowered to the surface of the desk to avoid her gaze in an almost shameful manner. "Exactly where he was from, we were unable to determine."

"What of his motorcycle? It should have registrations." "Stolen. I know what you're thinking," he sighed, throwing his arms up in the air, "and yes, I took a chance with doing it, but some of the patients would have died if they did not get a transplant anytime soon, and then this happened, his organs being intact, and functional. I took it as a sign."

"The only times you are supposed to look for signs is when they are displayed as symptoms," Marie hissed as if she was trying to exhale poison at the man she had lost all respect for, who had gone from being the person she looked up at the most to being absolutely nothing to her. You could see it on the twitch of Vernon's muscles by the corner of his mouth that he did not like it how she spoke to him as if she were above him, but he had done pre-rookie mistakes that were without any excuse, so Marie would not waver. "We need to inform the authorities," she then continued. "We don't if whatever this is can spread, neither how it would if it does. This could get turned into an epidemic fast if we don't act now, and there is still chance to stop this if we are lucky. Who were the other patients who got transplants?"

As if on cue the phone rang beneath the papers. The two shared a glance before Doctor Vernon began to dig through the pile in order to get to the phone, and pressed a button to get it on speaker.

"Doctor Vernon's office."

"Andrew..." came from a raggedy voice on the other line, sounding absolutely drained of all energy. It was only for the fact that the caller addressed Doctor Vernon by his first name that Marie was able to deduct that it was his wife calling, since the way she sounded now she could barely recognise her. The last time she saw her it had been at a benefit concert, and more importantly heard her ordinary, joyful voice which did not sound anything like this foreign voice sounding like an eighty-year-old woman who had been a chain smoker since she was fourteen. "I'm not feeling well... When will you be home?"

"You didn't..." Marie breathed, and suddenly it went up for her, made sense why Doctor Vernon had done what he had done. It was just as stupid with or without reason, yet Marie was able to understand his reasoning more now, though she did still not agree with his decision. Sweat was beading on the man's forehead, the lacking of a reply being more than enough of an answer.

"I'll be home right now, love." There was a tremor in his voice, making him be on the verge of breaking out in stutter. "Don't worry, just stay there, and–"

"Hello, darling..."

Both Marie, and Doctor Vernon furrowed their brows in wonder, intently listening to what was happening on the other end of the line for some explanation to the turn the conversation had taken. "Elise?" Doctor Vernon finally questioned, about to repeat his wife's name when the words kept coming, but what was said made the shade of his already pale skin grow even paler, the drops of sweat slowly cascading from his temple, and down his cheek to hang off his chin.

"Hi, Mommy!"

All Marie could do was to stare at the phone, frozen in her stance, as if she had gazed upon Medusa herself. She needed to hear how

this would unfold, feeling her heart pulsate all the way up in her throat. Marie could not speak a word to Vernon, but knew that what was going through her mind had undoubtedly already coursed through his by the time she had finished her thought. Their daughter didn't sound like she could be older than five, and had that blissful, juvenile ring to her voice in the sheer love she harboured for her mother.

"Come to Mommy, my sweet."

"Are you all right, Mommy?"

"Of course… I'm just tired."

"You should sleep, and I can take care of you!"

"My sweet little darling. Always so… so helpful." His eyes came to flicker up to Marie's, who broke contact with the phone to change her focus to her colleague. The only thing he did was to stare at her with a pleading look, all signs of fear and desperation eminent on his features, like he wanted her to come up with an idea that would save the situation, but she had no answer for what to do. To go to their house would take too long, knowing that Doctor Vernon lived at least forty-five minutes away, and she knew no words to speak here either that would help either of them. While hearing giggling from his daughter Leah, they stood there like a couple of fools, wishing for the other one to know what to do, or at least be as bright so they could be able to figure it out before it was too late. Their gazes averted from one another's when the husky voice of his wife began again in an almost singing tone. "This little piggy went to the market. This little piggy stayed home."

"Elise, you need to listen to me," Doctor Vernon tried in his sheer desperation of what might occur if he did not manage to intervene soon, leaning his body over the phone like a shrivelled plant, with his hands holding onto both sides so intensely his knuckles whitened under the pressure. "Let Leah go, you need to let her go, and I'll come home, and take care of everything, just put her down, please, put her down!"

But his words went unheeded, Marie wondering if his wife was still holding onto the phone, or if she had placed it down somewhere when their daughter came along to direct her attention there instead. In that case Doctor Vernon would not be heard, and it would be futile no matter what he said to the phone.

"This little piggy had jam and bread. This little piggy had none. And this little piggy went crying…"

"Elise, no, please don't do it! Listen to me, you need to listen to me!"

"All…"

"She's your daughter! Leah! Leah, can you hear me!?" "The way…"

"Leah, run!!"

"…To town."

The End.

Case #60782
Rayne KaaHedberg

My name is Rayne, and the world of fiction has always been my home.

Currently, I am a student of the humanism courses, focusing on culture at a *gymnasium* (the Swedish equivalent to the American high school) of Malmö, which is located in Skåne in the southern parts of Sweden. My studies have included courses such as culture-history, Latin, Japanese, as well as mandatory Swedish along with English that I will study in a course called *Cambridge English* during my third year. Although I am Swedish, my parents raised me to be bilingual, and I have therefore found it simpler to express myself in English rather than in my native tongue.

When it comes to writing, it is a passion of mine that I would someday like to move past the hobby stage to have it be my source of income, seeing as how much I burn for this. Writing has always been close to my heart, since it is about telling a story, and I have always loved stories in any way shape or form. Whether it comes to an oral tale, a story in a video game, a comic, a film, or in a book it never ceases to mesmerise me when being told a good story.

So on my spare time, when I don't write or study (or sleep) I spend it as a sponge, absorbing inspiration, and knowledge through books, films, and so on, expanding my pool of ideas to later piece together in different stories if I am able. In my time I have no clue of how many films I have actually watched, and as for books it ranges from old Shakespeare to today's Stephen King with a lot in-between.

This is the first time I have tried to send something in, and was as lucky as to get accepted, which in itself is such an incredible boost for my sometimes awfully faltering self-esteem. As for the future, there are no made plans for me to stop, since still so many stories only wait for their time to be told. Furthermore, I will continue to try and spread my work with this achievement as my beginning. The world of literature is a vast one, not in the least incredible, and I want to be part of it.

CLAYTON HILL SANITARIUM

The Inbox

Anthony Hanks

Physician: Dr. Peterson
8268-WCT29

*H*AMLIN CAN KISS MY ASS! Kim thought. Dumping this much work on her (or anyone at Olek Transportation) after the week she'd had wasn't just an asshole move, but in Kimberly Litner's opinion it was morally wrong. It had only been five days since the company's manager of order fulfillment had wrapped his BMW, as well as himself, around a tree. Hell, it had only been *two* days since Kim and the rest of Olek Transportation (O-Trans to their clients) had seen their manager of order fulfillment lowered into the ground. *Hamlin should have given us the week off. We're not that big of a company.*

Frank Hamlin, however, felt differently. He thought a four-day weekend was plenty of time to mourn for the loss of Paul Ambrose, and that company business must move forward.

"If we're not moving forward with the business, it's as if we're dying right along with him," he'd told Kim when he called her into his office. And then, just to hammer home how clueless he was when it came to social conversation, "Paul wouldn't have wanted that."

"I understand," Kim lied.

"Good," Hamlin continued. "Now we need to get the ball rolling on this refund project."

Mr. Olek wanted O-Trans to take a "No Refunds" approach to the company's rental contract. Up to that point, many of the company's larger clients--like hotel chains--signed a one-year contract for limousine service, and they paid monthly. At the end of that year the clients went on a month-to-month contract renewal and continued paying. However, many didn't realize this so they didn't bother calling for service after their initial year was up. Months later Kim's team would be bombarded with refund requests for unused months. Historically the company had no problem issuing refunds.

Not anymore.

Olek Transportation was cutting expenses wherever it could, and denying refunds for unused services was now at the top of the list.

"This is a shitty call, I know," Hamlin said, "but it's over my head so we just have to deal with it. Now, what do you think it's gonna do to the complaint department and new sales?"

How should I know? Kim thought. *I'm not a mind reader, and we don't even have a "complaint department."*

"I really don't know," she said. "I mean, of course it's going to cause an increase in complaints, but there's no telling to what extent. As for new business, I think the impact will be much less drastic. We probably just need to rewrite the verbiage on our sales contracts so that we're crystal clear on our auto-renewal and NO REFUND policies."

Hamlin shook his head. "I don't want to mention the phrase *NO REFUNDS* in the contract. It could scare a lot of buyers away." He had made quotation marks with his hands and fingers when he'd said "NO REFUNDS." Kim hated him when he did that, and he did it a lot.

Look, you prick, why don't you let me get with everyone else and give them a heads up, she thought. *Then we can come up with a worst-case scenario plan and give it to you so you can pick it apart like you do with every other fucking thing.*

"Tell you what," Hamlin said, "why don't you reach out to the other supervisors and get an idea of what this is gonna mean for each team, then you all can put together a plan for me to review?" Kim wanted to stab him in the heart with the letter opener sitting

on his desk. "I think that's a great idea," she said.

Hamlin grinned, his nicotine-stained teeth shining like little kernels of corn. "Great, I'll let you get to it then. Why don't you set up a meeting for tomorrow afternoon and you can all present your recommendations?"

WHAT?!? Twenty-four hours to put all this together?!? Kim's eyes once again darted towards the letter opener on Hamlin's desk, but she didn't reach for it. Instead, she said, "Well, I guess I'd better get back to my desk and get started then."

"Okie dokie. Thanks for taking the reins on this one, Kim."

Like you gave me a choice. Kim got up from her chair and turned to walk out of Hamlin's office. That's when he cleared his throat.

"Oh, and Kim...I'm sorry about Paul. I know you two were... close."

Kim stopped dead in her tracks. She could feel the accusation in his tone, and if she'd still been sitting, she probably *would* have gone for the letter opener this time. Kim spun on her heels and stared at Frank Hamlin, who hadn't even bothered to go to the funeral. "No. Not really. We went out a couple of times but that was it."

Hamlin flashed his corn kernel grin again. "Oh. Well I'm sorry at any rate."

"Thanks." It was the only thing she could think of to say. Kim walked out of Hamlin's office battling a maelstrom of emotions. She *had* been close to Paul Ambrose for about three weeks, right after she'd started with Olek Transportation. She'd told Hamlin the truth when she said they'd gone out a couple of times. Kim had even made the horrible mistake of sleeping with Paul after the second date.

And that's when she realized he was a total asshole.

He'd gotten into her pants (pretty easily actually) and that was apparently all he'd been after. The next morning Kim had been standing in his kitchen wearing nothing but panties when a woman walked in from the garage. The woman turned out to be Paul's wife, returning home early from a business trip.

Paul never slept with either woman again. His ex-wife got half of his money. All Kim got was a nasty set of bruises on her ass where he'd been a little too rough the night before.

That had been two years ago and since then Kim had done a fine job of ignoring Paul Ambrose and his sporadic sexual advances, and an even better job at hating him. After one particularly inappropriate conversation in an elevator, Kim had gone to her company's Human Resources department and filed a formal complaint against Paul. An investigation was launched and he was suspended without pay for 10 days. Kim had received a threatening text during that hiatus from an anonymous number, which read *"you ruined my marriage cunt but you won't ruin this."* Kim knew it had been sent by Paul, and she went back to Human Resources, but they told her they had no proof that it had been sent from him. To make matters worse, Paul returned to work the following Monday.

He only lived another five days after that.

Strangely though, when Kim finally arrived back at her desk, she couldn't help but feel a pang of sadness at the thought of Paul's death. The feeling only lasted a moment, and she was unable to suppress that darker side that was secretly glad he was dead.

Kim dropped into her chair and slid far back into the recesses of her small cubicle, wishing like hell that she had an office with a door she could close. For a moment she was able to force all thoughts of Paul Ambrose, their affair together and his death from her mind. Instead, she focused on the daunting task of getting multiple members of the company's management team together and on the same page with what had to be less than 24 hours' notice now. Kim glanced at her watch, just to confirm *exactly* how much time she had.

Jesus! It's ten after five! Most of the people she needed to talk with were probably already gone, and they wouldn't see any emails from her until the following morning. *Hopefully some of them have their emails forwarded to their mobile phones; at least some will see it tonight.*

Kim let out a long sigh and decided that the longer she waited, the more impossible her task was going to become. She slid halfway out into the aisle and looked around the sales floor. There were a few team members still at their desks, but mostly what Kim saw was a sea of empty cubicles and blank computer monitors, although some were flashing personal screen savers with photos of kids, husbands, pets and for the lonely single people--like Kim--a few "friends at the beach" pictures.

She rolled back in and opened up her email application. She opened a new message, cracked her knuckles and began to type:

Team,

As some of you may have heard, we've been given a directive to institute a "no refunds" policy effective by the end of the week. I met with Mr. Hamlin today and he's asked that we all get together and come up with contingency plans as to how this is going to affect our respective departments. We have to have these plans in place by close of business tomorrow. Sorry for the short notice. Look for a meeting request to follow this email soon.

Kim then searched the company's online directory and found an empty conference room that she could book for their meeting the following morning. Then she scrolled through her contacts list and selected "Distribution List: Managers" so that each department head received her email and the meeting request. She selected the option for a "read receipt" so she'd be automatically notified when the other managers had read her emails, and then she clicked SEND.

Kim barely had time to slide back from her desk before she started getting "OUT OF OFFICE" replies from her coworkers.

Most simply said they were gone for the day and they would be back Thursday morning. One reply, however, made Kim sick to her stomach.

From: Ambrose, Paul

Thanks for your message. I will be out of the office, with limited access to email, until Monday, October 17th. I'll respond to your message as soon as I can.

Thanks, and have a great weekend!

He would have activated this around five o'clock last Friday, Kim thought. *Barely seven hours before he died.* Kim's eyes began to sting and she was once again confused by her own emotions. She wasn't sure if the threat of tears was caused by anger or sadness. She deleted Paul Ambrose from the Manager's Distribution List, just like the blind curve and large oak tree had deleted his existence from the world.

The guilt of hating a man that hadn't even been dead for a week was stressing Kim to the point that she felt she could burst.

Christ, I need a smoke.

Kim was working on quitting and had managed to cut back to about four cigarettes per day, usually while she was at home. She kept a pack in her purse though, for those times during the day when she was feeling particularly irritable.

Today certainly qualifies.

Kim took the elevator down to the first floor, and started making her way to the rear entrance of the lobby. She stopped in front of the last office before the exit doors. The lights inside the office were out, just as Paul Ambrose had left it last Friday. Kim was wondering if and when the company would clean out all his stuff. After what felt like ages, she continued out the back door, to a place everyone called the "Suicide Lounge" and had her cigarette. When she came back inside, she managed to make it all the way back to the elevators without looking at Paul's office.

The cigarette hadn't done much to calm her nerves, and as Kim stepped off the elevator back on the third floor she wished that she'd had a strong drink to go along with the Marlboro. She headed back to her cubicle and before she took her seat, she glanced around the sales floor again. Everyone had left for the day and Kim had the office to herself. The Fall sun had dipped down behind the surrounding buildings, and the only light in the office was a few overhead fluorescents and the occasional screen saver, as well as Kim's own computer monitor. Kim realized just how creepy the empty office could be at night when compared to the hustle and bustle of the normal daily floor operations.

Screw it, she thought. *I've done everything I can for today. I'll come in early and get ready for this fiasco in the morning.* She sat down and began closing out of the applications she had open on her desktop. She started to click out of her email app when she noticed she'd already received a few "read receipts" and replies to her email and meeting request. *Must have come in while I was smoking.* Kim quickly scanned the replies she'd received. There were a few pre-emptive inquiries about the details of the "no refund" project, but mostly they were just read receipts. Kim was just about to close out her email when there was an audible *PING* and a new read receipt popped into her inbox.

Kim suddenly couldn't breathe. She rubbed her eyes so hard she saw stars behind the lids, and then she looked at the auto-generated message again.

Ambrose, Paul has read your Email sent on 10/19/11 at 5:58 pm. *That's impossible. This has to be an I.T. glitch.* Kim had almost convinced herself that this was true when there was another *PING* and a new email from Paul Ambrose popped up in her inbox. There was only one word in the subject line: "**hello.**" The body of the email was blank. Kim began to shiver uncontrollably, and she could feel her heart pounding in her chest like a prize fighter working over a heavy bag. She stood up and surveyed the sales floor again, looking for some sign that she wasn't alone. All she saw was the same familiar, and now terrifying glow from a handful of computer monitors. The office suddenly seemed five shades darker than when she'd gotten back from her smoke break. There was no question that Kim was alone on the floor, sitting mostly in the dark and receiving emails from a dead man. Kim's fear started to transform into frustration, mostly at herself.

This is insane, she thought as she sat back down in front of her computer. *Paul Ambrose is dead and buried and there's no way he could be emailing you right now.* Another *PING* sounded from her computer's speakers, indicating a new email had come in. It was from Paul.

Once again there was only one word in the subject line: "**kim**." Kim clicked on her name to open the email, and she expected it to be blank like the first one. It wasn't.

i know urthere

Kim wanted to scream, and even tried to, but no sound came out. She couldn't remember the last time she'd been so terrified. *Should I call after-hours security? And tell them what, exactly--a dead guy I screwed once is emailing me?* The thought of being hauled off in restraints to a mental institute helped suppress the fear again. *Somebody's screwing with me.* With a shaking hand, Kim moved her mouse and directed the cursor on the screen until it hovered over "REPLY." She clicked it, and started typing.

Who the hell is this?

She clicked "SEND" and this time she wasn't surprised when there was another *PING* almost immediately. She opened the email and read the response to her question.

paul

She started typing again, faster this time.

BULLSHIT! WHO ARE YOU!!!!!!!!!!!!!!!!!!!!!!!!!!!!!!!!!!
She clicked "SEND."
PING

your fuk buddy. lol

Kim did not "laugh out loud." Instead she started to cry, partially from anger, but mostly from fear. She typed.

YOU SICK FUCK!!!!! YOU HAVE TO BE REALLY MESSED UP TO DO SOMETHING LIKE THIS!!!!

PING

nasty mouth i can think of betterways to useit naughty littledevil

The last part of the message halted Kim's typing.

My tattoo.

It might have just been a coincidence, but Kim's instincts were telling her differently. Her freshman year in college was the year Kim decided to work out all of her pent-up frustration developed as a result of her folks' strict parenting. In other words, she was a wild-ass. That was the year she got a tattoo of a little baby devil wearing a diaper. The tattoo was located in a place on her body that nobody in the office could have known about.

Except for Paul Ambrose.

He must have told someone, Kim thought, even though she didn't truly believe it.

PING Another message in the inbox.

comeon you know you miss me how about a quickie for old times' sake

There has to be someone in Paul's office, using his computer! I could call security and have them check------

PING This time it wasn't an email that popped in her inbox. It was a meeting request.

Organizer: Ambrose, Paul
Subject: my cockyour mouth
Location: kims desk
Meeting Time: 6:08pm-6:13pm

Kim glanced at the clock on the bottom of her screen. It said 6:06. Her heart started up again with its prize fighter pace and for the first time she was scared of something more than seeing a ghost. She was scared something or someone was going to hurt her, or worse. She grabbed her purse and quickly rummaged through the contents until she found her key chain with the small canister of Mace attached to it. It was a gift from her overprotective brother and the can had "Zombie Spray" on the label. *If it will work on Zombies it should work on ghosts, right?* Kim shook her head. *Don't be crazy, it's got to be some perv screwing with me.* Either way, she was suddenly overcome with an almost overwhelming sense of love for her paranoid brother. *Fuck it! I'm not waiting around to be a victim.* With that, she got up from her desk and slipped her heels off so she wouldn't make any noise when she walked. She took off in a silent run towards the elevators, carrying only her keys and her Zombie Spray.

I'll get my shoes tomorrow, if I'm still alive.

Kim got to the lobby and quickly pressed the elevator call button.

The doors to her left opened and she stepped inside, pressing the button for the first floor. What Kim didn't see was the second set of elevator doors--the ones on the right side of the lobby--open.

She also didn't see the strange, wispy mist drift gently out of the elevator and into the hall. Hector, the company's day security guard, would see it on the camera footage the next morning, but he'd think it was just an anomaly on the recording. Neither Hector nor Kim saw or would see the strange mist drift onto the sales floor. None would see the mist knock over random family photos on desks, just because it could. Finally, not a soul would see the mist hover over Kim Litner's desk and eventually take on the shape of the late Paul Ambrose.

Two floors below, the elevator doors were opening and Kim stepped out. The first-floor lobby was identical to the one on the third floor but somehow it was different down here.

Jesus, it's freezing.

Kim ran to the front doors of the lobby and shoved.

She stepped back in terror. The door handles were freezing-- cold enough that her skin almost burned when she touched them. The most terrifying thing about the doors was that they wouldn't budge, no matter how hard Kim pushed. That left only one other way out of the building.

The rear exit.

Kim exhaled, expecting to see her breath, but she couldn't. It wasn't *quite* that cold. She looked down the hall leading out to the "Suicide Lounge", where she had just smoked a Marlboro thirty minutes earlier. Paul Ambrose's office was at the end of the hall.

Right where I left it.

There was no way to get to the rear doors without whatever was in Paul's office seeing her. Kim took the plastic safety pin out of her keychain of Zombie Spray and started tip-toeing closer to Paul's office. *Oh please let it be a zombie. Or some perv from receiving. Just don't let it be Paul.* She stopped in her tracks for a moment, visualizing Paul sitting behind his desk, typing dirty messages to her, his face and upper body a mangled road map of torn tissue and coroner's stitches, his lower body pretty much intact, including his penis which--in Kim's mind--was fully erect at the thought of violating her.

Kim was snapped out of her necro-rape fantasy by a horrible sensation. The can of Zombie Spray was slipping from her fingers.

She quickly fumbled with the can like a little leaguer bobbling an infield fly and eventually clutched it to her chest before it could hit the floor, alerting whatever retched thing that was in Paul's office to her presence. When she was finally able to breathe again, Kim crept forward until she was just outside Paul Ambrose's office door. She exhaled deeply and now she *could* see her breath. Kim brought her can of Zombie Spray up in front of her, said a silent prayer to a God she hadn't consulted in years and stepped into the office, expecting to see Paul's corpse sitting at the desk, waiting for her.

Paul wasn't at the desk. Neither was a perv from receiving or a zombie. The room was the same as it had been when she'd walked by it half an hour earlier.

Only it wasn't the same.

The office had been pitch-black inside when she'd gone out to smoke, and now it was washed in an eerie blue light coming from the computer monitor on the desk. And it was cold; so cold that Kim had to wrap her arms around herself and still couldn't keep from shivering uncontrollably. She should have been relieved that nobody was there to attack, rape or kill her, but Kim was more frightened at that moment than she had been when the emails started coming in.

What is going on?

She stepped further into the office, slipped behind the desk and finally stood in front of the computer monitor. She stared down at Paul Ambrose's inbox, and at the email trail that she had--just 5 minutes earlier--been engaged in. Without even realizing she was doing it, Kim reached down and touched the keyboard. She quickly jerked her hand back as if she'd just touched a hot stove top. Only it wasn't heat that made her recoil, it was extreme cold.

PING

Kim screamed at the sound of the incoming email in Paul's inbox. When she was sure she wasn't having her fifteenth potential heart attack that day Kim looked at the email that had arrived. Kim actually laughed a little when she saw who the sender was.

"Litner, Kimberly" was flashing at the top of the sender list in Paul's inbox. Kimberly Litner clicked on her name and read the email.

naughty littledevil im at your deskand urnot but i know where u r

PING Another message from *her* desk.

no worries im on my way back down youcunt then i will tear yourass apart

Kim might have made it if she'd ran, but all she could do was move slowly away from the computer. Eventually she walked backwards out of the office and into the hallway. There was no telling how far Kim would have walked backwards had the sound of the descending elevator not stopped her. Now Kim's laugh was more maniacal--a high pitched wail that finally tapered off when she ran out of breath. *Why would a ghost need to use an elevator?*

She never got the chance to ask.

The bell dinged and the right-side elevator doors opened. Kim stared in horror as a wispy mist drifted out of the elevator and into the hall. Hector the security man wouldn't see this part the next day, because, as he would tell the detectives five days later, "the recordings got all messed up after Ms. Litner got in the elevator on the third floor."

The mist started to take on a familiar shape, beginning with a grin that Kim had learned to hate.

After that, Kim Litner began to scream.

The End.

Case #90226
Anthony Hanks

Anthony "Tyson" Hanks is a fan of horror—both literature and film. He wrote quite a bit when he was younger but was struck with a tragic case of adulthood. He has recently taken up the hobby again and is thrilled that some folks have deemed his work worthy enough to show the public. He has yet to receive a literary award, but he did get a gold star on a middle school English paper once. His work has previously been published in *Sanitarium Magazine*, and will appear in the upcoming anthology "Kneeling in the Silver Light." He lives in Florida with his beautiful wife and daughter, and when he isn't writing fiction, fishing or working the dreaded "day job" he--along with a couple of fellow horror nerds--writes film, book and haunted attraction reviews and articles for their horror blog www.nerdcronomicon.com .

CLAYTON HILL SANITARIUM

Twenty-Four & A Bottle of Rye

Adam Kennedy

Physician: Dr. Edgar
9328-SJE41

I'M GOING TO DESTROY MYSELF WITH BOOZE.

Why the hell not? In every bottle there are a thousand dreams. Dreaming is a lost art these days. You won't find dreams being had on Tumblr or Reddit. Memeing has killed dreaming, in a way. The more we train our minds to accept the repetitive and the familiar, the minor alterations, the more the bold and the furious rebellions frighten and alienate us. That is why I drink. To make the alien familiar again.

Call me Maxwell. I pull bodies up from the bay after they fall off the Golden Gate Bridge. You'd think it's disturbing, but it's not. I understand why they do it, the jumpers. The world is becoming a labyrinth. For some of them jumping is the only way they can find peace. The fall, of course, is terrifying. The few who have survived all say that. But there has to be something about dying with the most beautiful city in the world staring you in the face, something spectacular that makes it worth it in the end. Otherwise, they wouldn't keep doing it. Twenty-four a year.

I don't think of the rest of them as often as I should when I drink. They were people, too; beautiful, each an endless library of stories, of dreams unclaimed. When I do remember the others, bloated and pale as the moon, it isn't pain or regret I feel… only a fleeting curiosity. None of them could be talked out of it. The ones who can don't jump.

At least, that's the way she explains it.

I've been a Marin County Coroner for six years. I've worked the Bridge for three. I don't remember the faces, except for one… hers. You may find that odd, but the reality is one human face becomes hard to distinguish from the next once it's been in the Bay for more than ten or twelve hours. I'd like to say we find them all, but the ocean was the first god of this world for good reason. It has a will we can't comprehend. They wash up on the rocks, Fort Point, or Crissy Beach. Sometimes they sink and get swept out to the Pacific side if they're still alive after the initial splash. The dead float better than the living… and it's hard to tread water with a shattered spine.

They belong to all walks of life. Whites, blacks, Asians, park rangers to hedge fund managers. They all come here to jump. To leap off into that blue abyss and feel true flight for the very first time, the liberation that always outran them in the labyrinth.

Her words, not mine.

Usually the crotch of the pants gets blown out on impact. Hitting water from that high up is, after all, like diving face-first onto a highway from a mile above. Not with her. She was naked when she jumped. SFPD found no signs of foul play. She had her bottom lip pierced with a ring, and barbells through her nipples and clitoral hood. She had big bedroom eyes and shoulder-cropped hair dyed neon blue. Pulling her onto the sand was the only time I can remember in the last three years that I've physically cringed in the field, like that deep, burning swig you've needed to take for years but that still burns you on the way down because you were never fully prepared.

She chokes up a laugh when I ask her why, says: "I was never meant for the ground. A free bird needs to fly."

It always feels wrong I can't see her breath. She was so cold. But the water running from the corners of her mouth... that seems right. The oily sheen on her skin. The Bay is as toxic and polluted as you can imagine, so the dead it gives back after they've fallen or jumped off the Golden Gate are usually well-intact and untouched by sea creatures. Her hair, matted and stiff like frost... her eyes. Oh God, her eyes. I prayed for a year about those eyes. The Catholic Church has made a fortune in quarters off those eyes.

When I catch them in the mirror, I start to wonder about her, I ask her things. Her eyes don't track their subject the way a living person's do. Like mannequin's eyes, they're just plain old-fashioned matter, nothing to animate or summon them to motion. And they'll always be there. Dead-straight and set on me, shining from a frigid, dune-white face. As predictable as the ratio of jumpers to months in the year. She watches from every mirror, every pane of every window, every puddle after it rains, every background of every call I make through Skype.

My wife gets nervous when I talk about her. "Max," she says (always with the Max), "You're scaring me. I think you need AA."

And I'll say, "I don't have the time. Within a week I'll have another jumper to deal with and I'm not even close to done booking the last one." As cyclical as a Bridge suicide, this argument unfolds. My wife can't see her. Part of me knows I can't either, in reality. But that doesn't make her disappear.

My wife hasn't seen what I have, doesn't know what's down there in the depths of the drink. My wife didn't pull a young girl out of the bay with black pools in her eyes and a lifetime of laughter silenced in a single gout of seawater trickling from her lips. My wife doesn't believe in ghosts.

There are wet footprints darkening the floor. I tell my wife I took a shower and didn't dry off well enough. I tell her the footprints are mine.

She asks, "How much have you had, Max?" to which I chuckle, then start to cry. She tells me, "This Hell you're in, you do it to yourself." Then she gets up to leave to go to the grocery store, says she needs to clear her mind.

And maybe she's right. Maybe I did ask for this, for the Bay to spit back its jumpers into every crack of my waking reality, when I chose this as my profession. But maybe it was the other way around; maybe it's they who chose me. They will still be there when the booze is gone. In the fleeting traces of my dreams, the flames of the church candles, in the ruddy silence of a long drive. It's only in drink that they come out into the open to tell me their reasons. And I will listen. Hers in particular, her with the piercings and the dyed-blue hair.

She's beckoning to me now, watching me from the door in the pale bloat of her eyes, a mere two steps away from where my wife just stood. She's been watching me the whole time, with a sad fascination in her gaze. She doesn't understand, I realize. Doesn't know why I try, or my wife puts up with it. Dead matter sees the world in ways the living never could.

She beckons again. She wants me to come with her. She wants me to fly.

"Free birds know secrets the caged ones don't," she says, a spray of oily black bay water spilling from her lips onto the floor. There is no wind in her voice box. Her voice sounds like a poem recited under the surface of a pool, vague and stutter-stop.

"No," I tell her, taking one long, last pull off the bottle. "Leave me alone. You're not real. I couldn't help you. You were already dead when I found you. You were already dead-"

The tears begin, a deluge, as they always do. The denial inherent to my mission statement is made clear in the rivulets drowning the stubble forest that patch my unshaven cheeks. I don't know. I never did. I don't understand any of it. Any of it, at all.

"Max? *Who* are you talking to?"

My wife's face peeks in the door. She was waiting outside, eavesdropping, or maybe she forgot her keys. The dead girl vanishes back down the neck of the empty glass bottle.

"Nobody," I slur. I kick the empty bottle under the bed. "You're scaring the living hell out of me." "Go to the store."

"Whatever you say…"

"Go. To. The. Store."

My wife's face disappears and the door clicks shut.

"Max." I hear the dead girl say, clotted words drifting through water. The pressure *pops* in my ears. She's close. I feel cold bay water running through my hair and down the side of my face when she speaks. "Max... Max. Fly with me, Max. Come fly. Think of all the *secrets*."

I fish the empty bottle out from under the bed and put in the recycling bin outside. I puke on top of a mountain of empty bottles. The dead girl doesn't speak any more for now. But I know I will see her again. And the others. Every one for a different bottle. The invitation of a hundred pairs of sightless, water-logged eyes.

I'll go to work tomorrow nursing the hangover I'm brewing, trying to push the images of her purple lips and pale gel eyes out of my mind's eye so I can focus on booking the latest poor soul who thought four seconds of free fall could liberate them from a lifetime of pain.

Then, in a week or two, another one will jump and I'll have to pull them from the steel blue maw of the San Francisco Bay. When it comes to bodies, the Bridge is an infinite giver.

Twenty-four a year. Twenty-four drowned deep in their bottles of rye. Twenty-four who fall because free birds should fly.

The End.

Case #95655

Adam Kennedy

Adam Kennedy is a game writer and designer from Northern California, currently living in Europe. He has a bad used bookstore habit, a love of redwoods, and a constant hankering for bluegrass. Since he landed his first gig in 2009, he has written stories for PC, console, casual, and mobile games. When he isn't working on one of those, Adam is traveling, reading a dog-eared paperback, or (slowly) finishing his first novel.

The Afternoon Show

Kanishka Narayan

Physician: Dr. Lotherton
8715-AED19

I WAS AT THE THEATRE AT 2:00 PM. My show would begin at 2:30. My friend had told me about this movie. It was supposed to be the movie of the century. It was said that the movie would break your soul. It was called "**Joy in Wretchedness**". You could not book your tickets online. You had to get your ticket at the theatre 30 mins before the show. I found that strange. Perhaps it was some sort of gimmick or marketing strategy to lure more customers. Just then, I got a call on my phone. I saw who it was. It was mother. She probably wanted to complain about the old age home again. That's all she wanted to talk about for the past few months. It really got on my nerves. She would always cry and tell me that abandoning one's mother was a sin. She refused to see the practicality, rationality of it. I decided not to pick up the call.

Anyway, I stood there at the theatre. I went to the ticket stall. The woman at the stall looked cheerful. She was dressed in yellow, which made her blonde hair look bright. She was wearing red lipstick. Her face was rather un attractive and she looked middle aged. She wore a cross on her necklace. She also had a tattoo of some Japanese character on her hand. She reminded me a bit of mother. I went over and said I wanted one ticket for the 2:30 show of '**Joy in Wretchedness**'. She looked up at me. She typed something in her computer and the ticket vending machine produced the ticket. "D-5.........to the right." she said. I was a bit astonished. I was not allowed to pick my own seat. "Could I have a different seat....a bit higher perhaps?" I asked.

"Huh........" She said looking back at me, "Sorry honey.........D5 is the only one available." She sounded very casual about it. I didn't know what to say. There were no other customers at the booth. I knew for a fact that there was no online booking available for this strange movie. " Excuse me Mam..........." I said. "I would like to see the seating availability on your computer"

She just smiled back and said, "Honey, that's confidential. Why don't you go wait outside the screen.......Your show will start soon."

I wasn't satisfied with her answer. "Mam, I know for a fact that there are other seats available. There's no one else here. Please let me just see what other seats are available." I asked hoping for a better response.

"You really don't know anything about this movie do you.........

Honey?" She asked as if she was mocking my intelligence. I did not understand what she was talking about. I just stood there dumbstruck. "When I said, D5 was the only one available, I meant D5 was the only one available **for you**....So please go wait outside your screen" She said. Now her stubbornness really reminded me of mother.

"Another gimmick" I thought. The marketing team for this movie was obviously fantastic. I decided I would play their weird game. I took my ticket, apologized to the woman and went toward my screen. I saw that other customers were lining up at the booth now. As I was walking away, the woman said in a loud and sarcastic tone, "Good luck honey..............YOURE GONNA NEED IT". I waved to her cheerfully. "Really good marketing" I thought. As I walked to my screen, I decided that I should get some popcorn. As I stopped at a stall and asked the boy running it to bring me one large popcorn with butter, he just gave me a puzzled look and replied, "I'm sorry Sir................there is no food allowed inside for this movie. Besides you won't feel that hungry." The marketing team had obviously gone all out. They had even got the popcorn guys to play along. I had to admit that I was impressed. I just went over to my screen and stood outside. There were other people there as well. There was an old couple, there was a businessman, there was a young teenage boy, and there was a fat middle aged man. It was 2: 25. The door opened, and a man stood at the door verifying everyone's tickets. As I handed mine to him, I asked, "Hey..........What's the deal with the seating...Huh.....?......Is there any particular order....or what?"

He looked at me. He was an old man, his eyes were red, his head balding, and his face weary. He looked like some kind of character out of a cheesy horror flick.........he said in his low voice, "Seating

is as per sins." "As per sins?" I did not quite understand what this meant. But I was amazed at the lengths to which these people had gone. They had even chosen the right words for the right kind of people. It was as if some casting director had been hired to pick out the right kind of people for the right kind of jobs. It was kind of creepy. Really good marketing.

As I went to my seat, I read the names of each of the rows. The first one was, 'A- Lust' The teenage boy seated himself in that row. The second was 'B- Gluttony'. The fat man seated himself in this row. The third was 'C- Wrath'. The old couple sat in this row. Finally, I reached my row. It said, 'D- Greed'. I took a seat. The businessman sat beside me. After a while, the lights were turned off. The murmurs in the crowd died down. The projector started playing the movie. The title appeared on the screen, **"Joy in Wretchedness."** There was no music of any sort that accompanied the title. The titles looked rather ordinary.

Suddenly, about 2 minutes after the titles, I heard some noises. I heard screams and wails from the rows behind me, I looked at the businessman. He looked as if he was glued to his seat. He sat there motionless, not a hint of emotion on his face. I was a bit freaked out. I wasn't even sure the movie had started. I looked behind me. From behind me the teenage boy screamed, " I'm sorry…………… …I'm sorry……….Il stay away from her……….I promise…… ……………….Just make it stop…………Please…….. PLEASE ………………...IL STAY AWAY FROM HER…….NEVER AGAIN …………..PLEASE." I didn't quite understand what was going on. This was turning into something macabre. The old couple started weeping now. They murmured something. Perhaps it was a prayer of some sort. I couldn't hear it clearly. From what I could hear, it sounded like the Jewish prayer for repentance. They wept, holding each other as if they were mourning something. Now, the fat man yelled as if his toe nails were being pulled out of his foot.

" No more cake for Larry…………I promise No more cake for Larry……………..I swear…………...NO MORE CAKE……………...I PROMISE…………JUST LET ME GO." If he wanted to leave so badly, why didn't he just leave? What the hell was going on?

Why were people screaming? Why were they crying? Were they also paid by the marketing guys? No, that would be too much. That's when I looked at the screen. There it was in block letters. My name appeared on the screen. I was petrified to see my name. Then the next scene showed me ….about five years ago….talking with my parents. I tricked them into selling me their house. It showed me putting them in an old age home. It showed them crying. Weeping for their son's acts. Worse than weeping. They were praying for their son's acts. Then it began again. It played the same scenes again and again. It brought back the memories repressed in my mind. I had betrayed my own parents. Tricked them for my own greed, for my own selfish interests. MY OWN GREED. I saw them crying on the screen. Suppressed feelings of guilt started to burst out of me. The guilt was too much. Feelings kept locked away, Questions kept locked away, came crashing out of my mind…..They demanded answers……..They demanded reasons………….I had none. I was alone looking at the past…..Looking at my deeds …………Was there a justification…………….

Or was I truly a monster? The scenes played again, again, and again……………Now I remembered why row D was called 'Greed'.

Now I understood why the woman had said that this was the only row available for me. The scenes played again on the screen. I screamed. I wanted it to stop. This Carnival of horrors. I wanted it to stop. This pain. It was too much. They said everyone has their demons. I felt like my demons were staring me right in the face, and they looked a lot like me. The scenes played again. There was an ugly face smiling at me. It was my face. It was too much. I tried to get up. I could not. It was like I was attached to the seat. I tried to move my arms. I realized I had no arms. I was attached to the seat. I yelled, I called out for help, and then I screamed again. "Oh God………Please someone……………..Just get me out of here …."

I screamed. The worst part was that I could not remember how I got here. I could not remember why I wanted to see this movie or the friend who'd told me to see it. I wanted to call mom. I wanted to apologize. I could not remember what day it was or what time it was. I was lost. The scenes played again. I could not remember my name. Who was I? What was I? I looked at the screen. I was the movie. The movie was me. I screamed till my throat went sore. Just then I looked at the seat beside me. It was the woman. The woman from the booth. There she was. Looking at me. Smiling her smile. There was something malevolent about that smile. "I knew you would need the luck honey………………….." She said and laughed aloud. I didn't know what the hell was going on. But then at that brief moment I knew. "HELL WAS GOING ON". There was no escape. I was alone with my guilt as I watched on screen the joy I sought in times of wretchedness.

The End.

Case #90803
Kanishka Narayan

Details not released
at this time.

Shopping

Luke Tarzian

Physician: Dr. Lichten
6428-SED41

IT'S FRIDAY, WHICH MEANS MOM AND I ARE GOING shopping. It's become our weekly custom: I get home from school, change out of my uniform and into a tank top and a pair of shorts, and then we're on our way, laughing about who ate shit on last night's *Dancing With the Stars* and wondering why Justin Bieber hasn't been deported yet. Seriously, the kid's a fucking asshole. But I digress. I was never really into *Dancing With the Stars* or celebrities with disposition issues, or really spending time with my mom in general. It just seemed like the decent thing to do when dad cut out and Billy passed away. It was my dad's fault, really; but he blamed my mom for his stupidity. I came home from school one day a couple years ago and mom was sobbing as if *Grey's Anatomy* had just been cancelled while dad talked to the officers and paramedics. Mom's antidepressant pills were on the coffee table in the living room; I guess Billy thought that they were candy because, according to the statement that my dad gave to the paramedics, he found Billy facedown on the carpet with a small, red tablet in his chubby hand—the only one left out of thirty. Dad, of course, blamed mom. They were her pills, he said, therefore it was her fault our little Billy died. What he failed to mention was the fact he was the one who left them out; that sometimes, when he thought no one was watching, he would crush the tablets up and snort them because he was fucked up to begin with. It wasn't mom's fault, it was dad's; it was his fault mom was on the ADs in the first place; it was his fault Billy died. Billy wasn't even five; he deserved a better father. My mom deserved a better husband.

Dad left a year ago. He took my mom's engagement ring and nearly all the money in her savings. She was hysterical. Not because of money (we had and still have plenty) but because she loved that ring. She showed it to me several times when I was little, said it was a star because it twinkled so much in the light. I thought it was pretty.

I hope it blows up and takes dad. That's what stars do, right? He deserves it.

We drive around town for an hour, window-shopping, looking, thinking, and then moving on because nothing catches our attention. Mom's extremely picky when we shop. We've been at this for three months now and we somehow always go home empty-handed. Sometimes I think we've found "The One", but after three days mom is usually in fits—it's not gold enough; its too small; yada, yada, yada—so we jump into the car (always on a Monday, it seems) and take it back to whatever store we found it at. It's all right, though; you can't rush perfection, and my mother's dead-set on obtaining nothing but the best.

We drive another thirty minutes before stopping at the park to rest. Mom parks the car and then we set off towards the center of the square. We find a bench and sit, watching people pass by, chattering like squirrels: high school couples; a few boys from my school; a blonde girl with a labradoodle; a mother with a king-sized stroller and two toddlers. Mom watches longingly as they walk by. I pat her on the shoulder and then take her hand; I can feel the sorrow, see it on my mother's face despite the fact she's smiling. It's an empty, hollow smile, though; she can't fool me. I've lived with her for sixteen years; I know her.

We sit in silence for some fifteen minutes before mom points out a family of ducks just near the pond. I laugh and watch the ducklings waddle. There are three of them, completely blond with little orange beaks and feet. They follow momma duck into the pond, eager to learn how to swim. We watch them for a bit before mom mentions that our little Billy used to love to feed the ducks. She sighs. I pat her arm and tell her we should go on with our shopping. She agrees and so we start back towards the car.

It's a little after two p.m. now. All the other schools are starting to let out. We drive past Lakeview Private and stop at a stop sign, waiting for the infantile gaggle to step onto the sidewalk. We drive another block, leaving Lakeview in our rearview mirror, and turn left onto Bridgeport Avenue, which—surprise, surprise—is home to Bridgeport Elementary. There's no one here, though, and I cannot help but think they must've had a pupil free day or that they got out early. The schools here run on different schedules even though they're in the same district. It's weird; and most of what I'm babbling about is pointless. Mom stops at another stop sign then continues on. The car slows down; I'm not sure why. I look at mom; her eyes are trained on something just ahead: a chubby little blond-haired boy in overalls, sitting on the sidewalk, crying. Mom parks the car and hurries towards the boy. He doesn't look much older than four or five. I get out too and look around. There's literally no one here: no crossing guards, no students, no parents—no one. Not even someone peeking from their house. It's a little fucked up. I mean, this poor kid's bawling his eyes out and not a single person's noticed—well, no one besides my mom and I. I look over at my mom, working to console the boy, who's got a cut along his knee. It doesn't look too bad, but you know little kids— everything's a big deal. Mom picks him up, still cooing in his ear, and walks slowly to the car. I tilt my head and follow, thinking that she looks a little happier. I get the back door on the driver's side and help her with the boy. Once he's settled in the car seat that belonged to Billy, mom and I both hop into our seats. The engine starts and mom looks at me a moment. I give her hand a pat; she smiles—beams, actually—and I can tell she's satisfied, that she has found perfection (temporarily at least; I know her). It's a bit messed up, but I know my mother needs this.

Besides, I've missed having a little brother. And if this one doesn't work out, then there's always next week.

The End.

Case #60946

Luke Tarzian

Luke was born in Bucharest, Romania in 1990 and has been writing since 2005. He's a graduate of the California State University of Fullerton, with a B.A. in English. He's an aspiring novelist, a lover of cats, and likes to indulge in a nice Jack and Coke every now and then. He firmly believes that Grumpy Cat is his soul animal. His favorite writers are Edgar Allan Poe and Neil Gaiman, and he is currently working on the second and third books in his "*Sewn From Seeds*" trilogy. His work has appeared in several issues of Sanitarium Magazine and his Dracula origin story, *Durante Lucus*, was recently sold to Alban Lake's *Blood Bond* imprint.

Luketarzian.wordpress.com
Facebook.com/rowesofficial
Twitter.com/luke_tarzian

CLAYTON HILL SANITARIUM

Bestselling Horror US

1 The Bird Eater - *Ania Ahlborn*

2 Pines (The Wayward Pines Series) - *Blake Crouch*

3 Bearing It All - *Lynn Red*

4 Wayward (The Wayward Pines Series) - *Blake Crouch*

5 Doctor Sleep: A Novel - *Stephen King*

6 Revival: A Novel (Pre Order) - *Stephen King*

7 This is the End: - *J. Thorn*

8 The Purge of Babylon - *Sam Sisavath*

9 The Shining - *Stephen King*

10 Innocence: A Novel - *Dean Koontz*

Compiled March 1st - March 31st 2014
Amazon.com Kindle Chart

Bestselling Horror UK

1 *Bearing It All - Lynn Red*

2 Bird Box - *Josh Malerman*

3 The Ghost House - *Helen Phifer*

4 Rejected By His Mate (Lycan Romance) - *M L Briers*

5 The Woman In Black - *Susan Hill*

6 Bloodstone - *Nate Kenyon*

7 World War Z - *Max Brooks*

8 Doctor Sleep: A Novel - Stephen King

9 The House on Poultney Road - *Stephanie Boddy*

10 Flesh and Blood - *Daniel Dersch*

Compiled March 1st -March 31st 2014
Amazon.co.uk Kindle Chart

Group
Therapy
04.14
Kraken Press, The Vampire
Queen and some great
reviews await.....

THE TEAM BEHIND KRAKEN PRESS ARE nearing the business end of their Kickstarter project for Aghast.

Aghast is a brand new, bi-annual, illustrated journal of dark fantasy and horror short fiction.

The publication, which will be released as an ebook and in print, will showcase short fiction that has a dark undertone. They have signed up with some great writers, including Jonathan Maberry, Gemma Files and Jeff Strand.

All of which have written stories exclusively for the new venture.

The illustrations are being looked after by the incredibly talented George Cotronis.

Here is a little from George:

"The first issue of Aghast is not yet completed. We have accepted one story so far and Megan Arkenberg and Tim Waggoner will be writing stories for our first issue. We are still accepting and reading submissions."

The Kickstarter project ends on the 29th April and has already hit its target of £1000 with 75 backers, showing that there is a love for the short story format.

it is however what happens after the dust has settled that I am looking forward to. We have seen magazines come and go and based on the preview issue (yes I am a backer of Aghast) I must say the look and substance of the publication makes waiting twice a year worth the wait.

Of course the Kickstarter may have finished if you are reading this after the 29th, however never fear - the Kraken Press team are working with some great writers in the horror genre to bring you not only Aghast but also a collection of original work in novella, anthologies and novel form. Richard Thomas and Max Booth III have work already available via Kraken Press and I am sure there will be many more to come.

   The level of detail that has gone into the covers, interior formatting and the depth of the stories themselves, prove that this is one to keep an eye on for the future.

Check out all the latest news over at their website:

http://krakenpress.com

Escape from Jesus Island
By Shawn French

Several months ago, I had the privilege of speaking with Shawn French about his upcoming comic book with Mortimer Glum called *Escape from Jesus Island.* At the time I couldn't help but think it was such a cool idea, and with Mr. French being such an all-around good guy, I hoped that it would take off and do incredibly well. My hopes came to fruition. The comic has garnered a lot of interest since its release, and rightfully so given its controversial subject matter, but most importantly it's become a sensation of sorts, and that's been showing with its popularity.

Well, it seems that things have come full circle to a degree as I first interview the creator before the books release, and now I'm reviewing issue one. How exciting. *Escape from Jesus Island* doesn't pull any punches with its title, for what you see is what you get. The opening panel features a bunch of college kids docking a boat on a terrifying looking island with one goal: To expose ReGen Corp's awful treatment of animals. Sadly, the group get more than they bargained for when they come face to face with dozens of failed genetic experiments.

The story is compelling and interesting, and it's truly the driving force behind the book. But that's not to say the artwork is of a lesser quality. Mortimer Glum's work is exception. It's drawn with such vivid qualities that the characters and environments often look like photographs. There's no use having a great story without having the matching artwork, and it's safe to say that Glum and French make quite the pair. Shades of Clive Barker shine through with several features, not least of all the gore and macabre. When doing a visual medium like a comic book or a movie, there's a fine line between being just right, or too much when it comes to the viscera and sinew, and I feel that *Escape from Jesus Island* hits the nail on the head, landing within centimetres of said line.

It's difficult to find many faults with the book, but I do fear that perhaps the confrontational topic may have gained a lot of interest at first, but it might falter down the line. It will be up to the creative team to keep people interested for as long as the comic's lifespan. People like to be shocked and awed, but at the same time the masses have been so desensitized to violence and controversy that they may become bored over time. Whether that will be the case has yet to be seen, but until future issues hit the shelves, *Escape from Jesus Island* #1 gets a full recommendation from me.

VERDICT 93%

Tortured Life
By T Publications

Alright, I would like for you to use your imagination for a second. Picture this: You wake up one morning, get ready for work, get
in the car or on the bus and for a second you see a dead cat in the street. However, you blink and you realize that the cat's not dead at all, it's sitting there doing cat things. You shake your head free of cobwebs, but in that time, the poor cat gets hit by a car, dead, exactly as you saw it. If you're anything like Richard in *Tortured Life*, you'd try to forget about. But what happens when these visions of death don't stop? Richard might think he has a solution, but at what cost?

Tortured Life is a comic book written by Neil Gibson, and in case you didn't get it from the short scenario up there, it's about a man named Richard Carter who, seemingly out of nowhere, can see the eventual death of everybody and everything around him. It's a chilling thought, and one that would be incredibly arduous to live with. It asks an interesting question of the reader, and implores them to search within themselves to compare their theoretical actions with the ones that Richard is actually making. The long and short of it is: The book asks a lot from the reader in a philosophical sense, which for a book that's ultimately about death, isn't overly surprising, even if it's not on the surface.

The premise is one that has been seen in the past, but I'm hard pressed to find a truly original story/plot/premise today. With that said, I think that *Tortured Life's* first issue is fairly engaging and interesting. It gives away a little and sets up a nice run, which is planned to be 6 issues. Needless to say, it will be exciting to see what comes next. With that said, the writing is pretty spot on too.

60

When I was reading it, I felt like it was an internal dialogue and not
just a narrator speaking over the frames, it was a nice touch, and it does take a fair degree of skill to pull off as a writer.

The artwork is good. I know that's very nondescript, but truthfully there isn't another way to put it. It does fit the story's atmosphere, but I feel it could have been done slightly better in the same style. On the other hand, it could have been much, much worse too. Like I said, it's hard to pinpoint where this falls in terms of skill and depth, but I feel it at the very least does the job. Art is very difficult to critique or judge, especially when I'm not an artist myself, but I can say I've seen worse artwork, and since it does fit the mood of the book, I can't argue with the choices made.

In the end, I would suggest *Tortured Life*. It was a great first issue, and it ends on a cliff-hanger, which only lends to the excitement of future issues.

VERDICT 87%

Andy Keep

The Vampire Queen

Where did the original vampire come from and how do you get rid of them?

Jessica Sawa, PA

Dear Jessica,

It is unknown where exactly the first vampire came from. Every Eastern European has their own history of the vampire. Bram Stoker's Dracula was supposedly based on a vampire. Some histories state that the vampire would return from the grave if he had unfinished business. Others would simply state they returned for blood so it is nearly impossible to pinpoint the first vampire.

As far as getting rid of vampires, there's the usual methods… sunlight, garlic, holy water, crosses, stakes through the heart, etc. You can do things to keep them in their graves like nail down their limbs, put rice or mustard seeds in the coffin (vampires have an obsession with counting), etc. However, the best and most assured way to get rid of vampires is to decapitate them and then set their body on fire. These are just the historically documents ways of ridding a vampire but now with all the vampire books out there I'm sure people have gotten creative and come up with some new way. Check out some books and see what you find.

There will be more from the Vampire Queen next month.

Also, we wish to say a very Happy Birthday to the Vampire Queen!

My Love Will Never Leave You

Kieron Hazel

Physician: Dr. Peterson
S268-WCT29

THE WOMAN LINGERED ON THE BRIDGE even though there was really nothing to see, just fast flowing water poisoned by pollution and a view of a distant chemical factory.

Grady watched her through the screen of undergrowth concealing the garbage strewn waste ground where he had made camp last night.

She was in her late thirties, Grady judged. Slender and fine-boned, her black hair gathered back from a heavily pockmarked face into a librarian's knot that accentuated the acne scars incised in her pallid skin. She wore a long overcoat despite the warmth of the mild spring day, yet still shivered convulsively, drawing the edges of the coat up under her chin as if chilled by an inescapable draught.

Grady felt as lost as she looked. He was walking home, at least that had been the plan, but who knew if he even had a home any more now that Jenny refused to take his calls. He had spent much of the previous evening listening to her old voicemails on his battered mobile phone while rain beat like divine torture on the sheet of corrugated metal he had turned into a makeshift tent. Grady had learned to take comfort wherever he could find it. Just hearing Jenny's voice made him feel a hundred times better than the drugs, the booze, all of the crazy shit that had landed him in prison. He had to make her understand that.

The phone in his pocket beeped, inspiring a surge of renewed hope until he remembered that the tone meant nothing more than a depleted battery. He withdrew the phone and looked at the cracked display for a moment, his reflection a gaunt, grey ghost in the dusty glass. He dropped the phone then stomped it into the dirt with the heel of his army boot.

Turning up the collar of his stinking combat jacket, Grady pushed through the flimsy partition of bush and stunted tree onto the path that led to the bridge.

***

Daphne's phone rang in her handbag. She closed her eyes and tried to will the sound away by harnessing the benevolent power of the universe. Positive images filled her mind, expunging fear, snapshots of her old life, a life before--

The phone fell silent before quickly announcing the arrival of a text.

Daphne reached into her bag as if it contained a starving rat and gingerly pulled out the mobile that monster had given her.

She opened her eyes and scanned his latest message: MY LOVE WILL NEVER LEAVE YOU x x x.

Tears spilled down her face. She could at least be grateful for this final intrusion; his words had strengthened her faltering resolve to do what had to be done.

A boot scraped on concrete behind her, terminating stealthy footsteps.

She spun around, anticipating the worst, but saw only a scruffy looking man in his twenties with eyes made large and wild by their vivid contrast with his grimy complexion.

"I'll take that," Grady said, holding out his hand for Daphne's phone. "And whatever else you might have in that bag. I'm sorry. I really am. It's just that I need what you have more than you do, so don't make this harder than it has to be by taking it personally and doing something stupid."

Daphne stepped back instinctively, only stopping when she collided with the bridge wall.

"Need? You have no idea what you truly need," Daphne snapped, glaring at him like an unmasked predator. "I pray you never do."

She turned to face the river and drew back the hand holding the phone like a slingshot.

"Trust me. This is for your own good," she said over her shoulder.

Grady's hand clamped her wrist before she could throw the phone into the river.

"Now that was stupid," Grady said, tightening his grip, wanting to hear her cry out.

Instead, seemingly oblivious to the pain, Daphne turned like a dance partner to face him. The mobile in her captured hand was close enough to Grady's face for him to read the display when the phone suddenly began to ring.

UNKNOWN CALLER, the phone indicated.

The ringtone was one Grady had never heard before, a mixture of electronic and organic sounds that somehow reminded him of mocking laughter. The sound seemed to twist in his mind like some feral horror struggling to escape from a sack. It wanted him to see something held beneath the dark current of his thoughts, a glimpse of his future now ready to float free...

Grady reeled from a blow to the side of his head.

He had closed his eyes. Why had he closed his eyes? Something about that damned ringtone ...

He let go of Daphne's wrist and stumbled back, feeling blood trickle down his right cheek.

Daphne held up the ringing phone as if Grady still had hold of her wrist. Her trembling left hand clutched a large stone spattered with Grady's blood. Daphne laughed hysterically. She slipped the stone into her coat pocket where it clinked against additional rocks of similar size. Grady registered her overcoat's bulging pockets for the first time and wondered dimly why she had filled them with stones.

Images pushed through the fog of his mind.

His head forced into the fetid depths of a prison toilet ...

Not fighting it ...

Taking away their power by willingly imbibing the vile slurry of shit and piss provided by a dozen malicious inmates motivated by too much time and too little entertainment ...

Willing to die just so long as the decision remained his to make. ...

Daphne's laughter ended with chilling abruptness.

"Perhaps this was meant to be," Daphne mused. "If some higher power led you to me then who am I to question its decision?" Daphne looked at the ringing phone and then back to Grady. "It belongs to you now."

Daphne threw the phone to Grady, who caught it reflexively. The jarring ringtone set off sonic bombs in his throbbing head. He gazed groggily at the display. UNKNOWN CALLER, UNKNOWN CALLER, UNKNOWN CALLER ...

His mind sang the words to the tune of the ringtone, mocking him like a despised song he could not shake from memory after hearing it on the radio.

Daphne was laughing again.

The sound brought Grady back to reality. He stood there, weaving on his feet, trying to summon the violence he needed to end this. Grady raised his fist but it hung impotently in the air as a bolt of pain skewered his head.

Daphne threw down her handbag between them and smiled at Grady.

"Maybe you do need this more than me," she said, then turned and threw herself over the bridge's low restraining wall into the river thirty feet below. Deranged laughter followed her all the way down.

***

Grady staggered back to his camp. Bile filled his throat whenever he moved his pounding head. He used the rainwater he had collected overnight to clean the blood from his face. There was a lump the size of an egg above his right ear, but at least that crazy bitch was in a worse state.

He sat down by the smouldering remains of his campfire. He had picked up Daphne's handbag, more by instinct than judgement, and now examined its contents after spilling them on the ground.

He cast an appraising eye over a diary, a purse, half a packet of mints, several used tissues, a set of house keys, and three books. The books consisted of two romance novels from what looked like a popular hospital series, and a self-help tract entitled UNIVERSAL LAW – THE POWER TO ATTRACT that had an envelope protruding from its pages like a bookmark.

Grady opened the purse. Thirty pounds in notes and some change. Enough to buy a train ticket. He pocketed the cash and threw the purse onto the bed of hot embers.

The only thing written on the envelope was the beautifully transcribed phrase To Whom It May Concern. Grady found a note inside written in the same painstaking hand.

If you are reading this then I am dead. Mother would call this the coward's way out. I'm sure she'll enjoy telling me that when death reunites us. Even so, I pray that it is indeed mother I find waiting on the other side and not the one who has driven me to this. Yours, in sorrow and shame, Daphne Morley.

Grady picked up the diary and began to skim pages.

I glimpsed him again tonight watching the house from across the street. He is always in shadow. So still, so silent. But even so, it thrills me that no man has ever looked at me in the way that I sense his unseen eyes do. He draws ever closer, but how close will he ultimately dare to come? I think there is something wrong with his

face. Is that why he keeps his distance?

A crow took flight nearby, startling Grady. He had killed a crow once after it had begun to plunder the patch of prison garden given over to his care.

It is like a vivid fever dream whenever he comes to me. Locked doors no longer keep him out. I worry Mother will hear us. Is it foolish to say that at last I feel like a real woman?

The crow wheeled overhead, caw cawing repeatedly as if calling for Grady's attention.

I am neglecting Mother. Even in her pitiful condition she realises something about me has changed. I never could pull the wool over her eyes, the old witch. That is the reason for her sudden, vicious resentment of me. No one likes to be reminded of their loneliness by someone they consider even more pathetic than themselves. She threw what happened with Father in my face when I took up her breakfast this morning. She said it was my selfishness that drove him away. I can barely stand to be in the same room with her now. Her stench disgusts me. I noticed for the first-time last night that he has the same smell.

Crows pair for life, Grady thought distractedly. For life ...

I found Mother dead in her bed today. It had been three days since I last looked in on her. Three days! The laughter I heard from her room had turned me into a child again, afraid to open closed doors for fear of finding them together. Doctor Bradley says I should try to get away for a while. He looks at me strangely now, a question in his eyes that we both find troubling.

So what became of its mate? Grady wondered distractedly as he turned the pages of the diary, remembering how snapping the neck of the great black bird had made him feel.

Whitby in October. Not so much a holiday as a return to the scene of the crime. I played on this beach as a little girl. Nothing much seems to have changed here in over thirty years. I have always loved the sea. Is it wrong to say I love it even more without Mother around to taint what little pleasure I can find in life?

The crow landed on the other side of the campfire and watched Grady while he read.

Last night we made love as frigid waves rolled over our bodies. It is not anything like the books. It is more a hollowing out than a filling up with something wonderful. Love is a cancer that is killing me, but slowly, oh so very slowly.

Grady felt the bird's eyes boring into him.

He takes everything. EVERYTHING. Soon even my reason will be gone. I do not think he is even alive. That is the worst thing. The most terrifying consideration. Because death may not bring release after all. If there is anything in our feeble humanity capable of surviving bodily annihilation then surely it is our desires.

Grady came to the diary's final entry and realised he had bitten his thumbnail down to the quick.

He whispers to me while I pretend to sleep. My love will never leave you ... My love will never leave you ... My love will never leave you ... Over and over and over again in a voice that makes me want to scream.

Grady shook his head, unnerved by the desperate horror of Daphne's life.

Something spooked the crow and it soared effortlessly into the sky once more, the sudden flurry of its huge wings fanning smoke from the fire in Grady's face.

Grady closed the diary and spat the taste of woodsmoke from his mouth.

He put the diary onto the fire next to the heat blistered purse. Its scented pages burst into sudden flame, reminding Grady troublingly of a curse that could not be taken back.

Grady picked up Daphne's mobile. An echo of her voice in his mind whispered tauntingly "It belongs to you now."

His thumb, bleeding from the masticated nail, inputted Jenny's number.

Have to make her understand, Grady told himself as he listened to the mobile trying to connect his call. If not me then no one ...

Someone picked up at the other end.

"Jenny?" Grady said in a choked voice, realising that at some point he had begun to cry.

Grady heard measured breathing over a light undertone of static. "Jenny, please talk to me. I know we can work things out if you just give me a chance to show you I've changed ..."

The breathing was louder now, more urgent, building to something, birthing a voice that struggled to break through with every exhalation.

Grady lowered the phone yet heard a sexless voice whisper "My love will never leave you," the sound like air forced through a lungful of dead leaves.

It was only then, when a hand oozing leprous foulness through a covering of sodden bandage came to rest on his shoulder with a squeeze that felt anything but reassuring, that Grady realised the number he had actually dialled belonged to the true love of his life.

The End.

Case #81863

Kieron Hazel

K. M. Hazel lives and works in West Bromwich, a post-industrial town in the dark heart of England. His fiction has been published in the magazines Gorezone, Samhain and now, at last, Sanitarium, a favourite haunt that shares his peculiar fascination with the dark side of human nature.

He cannot remember a time when he was not obsessed by all aspects of the horror genre. Formative influences were Hammer and Universal horror movies, the stories of Edgar Allan Poe, and the older brother of a childhood friend who traumatised him at a tender age with his secret stash of horror magazines. His love of horror is an interest that has troubled parents, educators, friends and employers alike over the years, but is an obsession he now lives easily with and no longer feels the need to apologise for.

The writers he most admires in the genre are Ramsey Campbell and Stephen King.

After a long time away from writing he has now returned to his first love and has numerous fiction projects nearing completion, details of which will shortly manifest at www.kmhazel. blogspot.co.uk

His main ambition is to write a story capable of inflicting serious psychological harm on the unwary reader.

CLAYTON HILL SANITARIUM

Yomi

Ben Welton

Physician: Dr. Peterson
8268-WCT29

"**H**EY, GEOFF. GET A LOAD OF THIS."

Harold Andersen was poking his fishing pole into the murky water off of Yomi Island. He hadn't caught anything all day, and frankly he was getting thirsty. He wanted the day to end so he and Geoff King could return to the shore and grab a few rounds at the Clam Shack. But the sight of the strange object floating in the water captured Harold's attention. He wanted Geoff's opinion for the moment, even though he knew that he was going to bring the item aboard regardless.

"Don't touch anything, Harold! You know as well as I do that there used to be a Navy base in these parts. There's no telling what they did back in the day."

"Aw, Geoff. Maybe it's something rare from the war. Maybe it's the very thing that'll make us wealthy. At the very least, it'll be the first thing I've caught all day."

"You're a plumb fool. I won't bring that rusty thing aboard for any kind of money, but I know you well enough to know that it's coming aboard no matter what I say."

Harold dipped his hand into the cold water and wrapped his fingers around the object. It was cylindrical, slimy, and it seemed to have two caps on both ends. It reminded Harold of those hard plastic containers that get shot up through the pneumatic tubes at the bank. When he brought in closer into the sunshine, Harold could tell that it was fairly old, possibly from either the 1930s or 1940s. On its side there were yellow numbers that had been stenciled in. Other than that, there were no indications whatsoever of the origins of the object.

"Boy, this is the damnedest thing I've ever seen. You figure it some old Army machine?"

"Don't know. Those numbers remind me of the ammo boxes that I used to lug around in Vietnam. Funny thing is that the nearest Army base is in Manchester, and that's a good hour away. If it's really Army, then how'd it end up here?"

"Maybe it's Navy then."

"Ain't been a government sailor in these parts since Korea. An object that lightweight should be in Africa right now if it had been pitched in during the '50s. Mighty strange, I'd say."

"Yep, you're right there. C'mon and help me open it."

Harold started pulling at the cap on the bottom end. He was attacking it like a jar of grape jelly, but the cap wouldn't budge. Geoff kept his hands away and tried to remind Harold that things found in the ocean should be left alone. Harold called him a "sissy" and again demanded his help. Reluctantly, Geoff put his muscles to work on the cap at the other end, and after a few minutes of struggling, both men got their respective opponents to budge a little.

Within seconds, a cloudy green mist appeared. It stunk something rotten, and its stench alone was enough to force Harold to the boat's port side. He began dry heaving with great force, while Geoff did his best to not breathe in the substance. With his fingers making a claw mask over his mouth and nose, Geoff fanned the mist away with his free hand. This got most of it to fade away, and after Harold joined in, the green mist completely disappeared.

"What do you think that was, Geoff?"

"I dunno, but whatever it was wasn't good. I think we better go ashore and see somebody."

"Right. And after that we're getting right and proper drunk at the Clam Shack."

***

"What are your thoughts on the supernatural, Mr. Bielagus?" Kent Orndorff was an obese man dressed in a too-tight suit. His shirt collar was open and it exposed his numerous chin rolls that all needed a shave. Orndorff's large office was equally disheveled, with papers, books, and maps thrown about. Liquid rings, which were mostly brown or black, were scattered here and there on his white desktop.

Conrad Bielagus was the exact opposite of Orndorff. Tall, lean, and cleanly dressed in a gray cardigan and khaki slacks, Bielagus looked every bit the military man that he used to be. A former NCO in the National Guard, Bielagus had earned a reputation as a sterling operator and a man who could get things done. Ever since ending his first career, Bielagus had started a second one in the world of private security. Often times this type of work put him into contact with less than savory characters, of which Orndorff was one. The fat lawyer disgusted him immensely.

"I don't personally believe in any of it. My wife believes in ghosts, though. But that's just because she watches too many of those ghost hunting TV shows. It's not healthy."

"Well, that puts your wife in with a lot of the country. My own wife hated them, and furthermore she hated me for thinking so highly of them. Maybe that's why she kicked me out."

Orndorff let out an awkward chuckle that belied inner anguish. As did so, his right had swept across the office as if to say "How do you like my new home?" Bielagus didn't give him and ounce of pity and he used his hard eyes to tell Orndorff to get on with it.

"I guess your skepticism is a benefit rather than a hinderance, Mr. Bielagus. And besides that, they tell me you're the best. I can only hope that the job that I am about to pitch to you strikes your fancy. It might prove to be adventurous, after all."

"My life has been pretty boring lately, so I'm sure that anything in the way of work should prove to be 'adventurous,' Mr. Orndorff."

"Excellent, excellent. Now, in order to prove to you that I'm not daft, I'd like to first explain why I asked you your opinions on the supernatural. You see, my little problem involves Yomi Island. You've heard of it?"

"Of course. That's where those Norwegian girls were murdered."

"Quite right. In the summer of 1884, Ann and Hannah Olafsson were killed with an axe by some unknown assassin. At the time, many of the island's more superstitious folks blamed it on the spirits of the Portuguese sailors who first found the island. They themselves were the victims of some unseen murderer, and like the Olafsson girls, they went to their graves unavenged. That makes for some angry ghosts, Mr. Bielagus.

"As for myself, I tend to think that Edward Myerson was the culprit behind the murders. He was a known vagabond, plus it was recorded at the time that previous to the killings he had sent love letters to Hannah, the elder sister. I came to this conclusion after reading Mrs. Wyman's excellent account of the crime, *Two Dead Souls*. Have you read it?"

"I'm afraid to say that I'm not much of a reader."

"That's a pity. Anyway, it's immaterial to your assignment besides the fact that both involve Yomi Island. I have a small cottage there, and recently I have been receiving strange correspondence from someone who claims to want something of mine. These letters have been threatening in nature, plus they seem to show an intimate knowledge of my art collection. I like neither of these facts, and I'd like you to put a stop of them."

"What do you mean exactly by 'art collection?' Are you speaking metaphorically, because I hate to say it, but the nature paintings in this room hardly seem worthy of theft."

"No, you're right. They came with the building. No, by 'art collection' I mean just that. As a man of means, I have traveled the world. In my travels, I have taken on the habit of acquiring local objects. In particular, my private collection specializes in those items that are supposedly cursed. You may scoff at this, but I can assure you that everything in my collection has behind it a dark past that is tied in with local and ethnic lore. I acquired the piece in question in Maine of all places.

"Last fall I was tramping through Chesuncook Lake and enjoying the wildness of the countryside. Just as the sun was setting, and thus turning the world from yellow to burnt orange, I discovered a jade figurine underneath some leaves and twigs. The absolute strangeness of the thing appealed to me immediately, and I could tell that it did not represent any craftsmanship from this or the previous century.

"After coming back home from my vacation, I took the figure to a local antiquarian who knows quite a bit about Native American art. At first I believed the item to be of Abenaki heritage, but the man refuted this, claiming that he had no idea where it had come from. He darkly hinted that the figurine might not even be North American in origin.

"That night I took it upon myself to closely inspect the thing. I too found it to be ghastly in a way that no Native American piece had ever struck me before. What it represented I could not clearly tell, but I guessed that it was some sort of aquatic deity. Furthermore, it presented to my eyes a somewhat humanoid form, with a face that looked Asian, specifically Central Asian. Either way, I must admit that it gave me the shivers.

"So accordingly, I locked it up in my private archive (which is now sadly in my wife's possession). By the time that I received the first letter, I had forgotten about the object's existence. Despite this, the menacing quality of these missives made me extra protective of the object. I am still protective of it, and that's why I would like you to go to Yomi Island and guard my cottage for the night."

"I guess I missed something, but if the object is in your wife's possession, then what is the point of my guarding your cottage."

"I'm sorry for not telling you sooner, but just last night I moved a large portion of my private collection to the cottage. I'm afraid you're going to have to keep that confidential for now."

"Okay, that makes out. One last question: where were these letters mailed from?"

"No return address or postmark. That's not a lot to go with, but that's where things stand."

"Well, if nothing else this will be the easiest $1,400 I've ever made."

"I hope so, and don't let the locals make you nervous."

***

"Man, I wouldn't be going to that island tonight. You're a brave man."

"It's a job."

The guy had been going on like this ever since Bielagus had rented his boat and his services to take him across the channel to Yomi Island. It was a thirty-minute ride, but to

Bielagus it felt like forever. The guy had started out talking about the Red Sox, then he flapped his gums incessantly about all the different suspects in the Olafsson killings.

"Yep, I think Shep Middleton is right when he says the governor did it. He needed an excuse to finally build a real police force on the island. Couldn't rely on the Pinkertons any more. Say, isn't that what you are - a private detective?"

"Private security. It's a little different."

"That's interesting work. Ever killed anybody?" "Not yet."

Bielagus's terse answer put the man off until the boat hit the shore. The coastline was sandy with grass and rocks sprinkled throughout. Ultimately it all came together to form a flat hill that represented the entire island. Bielagus stepped off and touched down on the wet sand.

"Do you know which one is the Orndorff cottage?"

"Sure do. It's the only building on the entire island. Can't miss it. Buddy, you're braver than I am. You know that's the house where those Olafsson girls got killed, right? Sure is a spooky place."

"You'll be here in the morning, right?"

"Yup. Six o'clock like you said. Take care now."

The small whine of the motor eventually became too soft for Bielagus to hear. By that point he had already made his way to the cottage's front door. It was brown and white with a thatched roof. In front stood a flagpole with an American flag on top. Using the light from the nearby lighthouse, Bielagus could also see that around the flagpole were a number of headstones.

They looked ancient and for the most part the names were indistinguishable. Bielagus could only make out one clearly - "Teixeira: 1809-1845."

***

After an hour or so of exploring the island, Bielagus settled into the cottage. He knew that he was completely alone, for the island had nothing else in the way of houses or even animal life. Seagulls would be loud in the morning, but that would be it.

Inside of the cottage, there was a fireplace, a two rocking chairs, a small TV, and a basic kitchen. The note on the refrigerator told Bielagus that it contained a few microwavable dinners and a couple of beers. A bottle of whiskey was on the counter, plus there was a coffee maker with a full coffee can sitting next to it. Bielagus made one of the dinners and fixed himself a pot of coffee with a little whiskey in it. He turned on the TV, but switched it off after only finding one watchable channel.

Bielagus began to pace the entire length of the cottage as he debated what next to do to offset his boredom. For a time, he tried to read a magazine, then read about three chapters of a paperback novel that was on the floor next to one of the chairs. It was a vampire story set in Civil War America. None of the characters were believable, and the author clearly had a fixation on Stephen King. Bielagus threw it down in disgust.

Sometime around two a.m., Bielagus decided to see the figurine for himself. Surprisingly, given the small size of the cottage, it took Bielagus quite a while to locate the item. When he did, he found it tucked away behind a few knick knacks in the cupboard.

The thing weighed about two pounds and was big enough for two hands to hold. It had a glow to it, Bielagus thought, almost as if it could be used as a torch of some sort. The face made him feel uneasy, for like Orndorff said, it seemed to be an unnatural blend of human and animal. Its rough form and ancient character also made him uncomfortable, and Bielagus told himself that he would be glad when the job was over.

The figurine, along with Bielagus, hit the opposite side of the cottage when the explosion tore through the house with a sudden and violent force. Even though concussed, Bielagus knew that the explosion had come from a localized bomb, probably a homemade IED of some sort. After gathering his senses, Bielagus saw that the door had been completely blown off. In its stead stood two men. Bielagus could smell them clearly, and they smelled like rotting fish. One of the men had a flashlight and the other had a revolver.

"All right now. You're coming with us and we're taking that idol." The man with the gun moved closer to Bielagus and put the muzzle next to his nose. The man with the flashlight swept next to Bielagus's side and picked up the figure. He handled it with care, almost as if it was something special to him. Bielagus had never seen crooks treat money or jewels like that, so he knew that he wasn't dealing with ordinary cons.

When he put the figurine into his breast pocket, Bielagus caught a glimpse of the man when the flashlight's beam went upwards. He was an old man in his sixties and his face was pallid to the point of looking green. He looked deathly sick, plus his gray eyes dropped and were circled by yellow crust. Bielagus assumed that the other man was likewise afflicted, but at least he had more spirit left him, for he grabbed Bielagus's arm with some force. He picked him up and forced Bielagus to walk in front.

Following the flashlight's beam, Bielagus caught on that the two men were leading him towards an old boat that was gently floating near the coast. It didn't have a motor, so Bielagus would not have heard their approach. Inside of the boat Bielagus could see a dark colored sack with a nylon chord.

"Get in and keep quiet. Grab those oars and row when we tell you to."

The man with the flashlight sat up front and used the light to track the boat's progress. The man with the gun sat behind Bielagus with the gun aimed at his kidneys. Only the man with the flashlight spoke, and when he did he gave directions."

"A little to the left now. Okay, pull us to the right and we should have it. Okay, Geoff. Let's get him in."

Bielagus brought the small boat to a stop at the entrance to a small cove. Across from them stood a cave's mouth that was blacker than

the night itself. Bielagus felt Geoff, the man with the gun, nudge him in the back.

"Pick up that bundle and follow Harold."

Bielagus now had both of their names. Geoff and Harold. Those names didn't automatically conjure up images of evil, but there was something morbid about both men. Typically, thieves kept their identities secret, but these two didn't seem to care that Bielagus knew their names. Besides this, neither one of them seemed agitated or otherwise alert. They moved automatically as if under a trance.

Within minutes all three men were inside of the cave. Bielagus, with the bag still in his hands, tried to guess what was coming next. By gently adjusting his fingers, Bielagus figured out that the bag contained candles, a box of matches, and some sort box that had wires attached to it. This then was the original bomb's brother.

"Take that bag and open it right where you're standing. Reach in and grab the candles. There's thirteen, so place twelve in a circle with one in the middle. Light them all when you're done. There's matches inside."

Bielagus worked slowly in order to observe his abductors. Neither twitched. The flashlight's beam remained focused on him, while the gun never wavered either. Bielagus had never been so scared in his life.

"Now that you've gotten everything ready, take out that box with the wires and place it in your lap. Sit Indian style."

Bielagus did as he was told and looked up at the faces of the men standing over him. Harold, the man with the flashlight, wouldn't make eye contact. Geoff, the man with the gun, would, and after locking eyes with Bielagus, began to talk.

"This island is a lot older than people think. We're still on Yomi, you know. We went around back to this place where the ancients used to come and worship him. Me and Harold found it one day. We had been fishing and we found this canister that contained a green liquid. We breathed it in. At first we thought that we had been poisoned. We called the doctor and we told our wives. No one knew what to do with us, so they gave us a lot of pills and put us on special diets. None of it worked. Before long both Harold and I were dead.

"I don't know how long we were underground, but when we came up it smelled like spring. While we were underground, we had visions. We saw things of the time before...the time before white men and even Indians. The people who used to live on this island came here before Egypt and Sumer. They looked like us except for the fact that they all seemed to be part animal somehow. That figurine that Orndorff found looks like one of them. The visions we saw told us to protect it. They also told us how to keep the island happy.

"It's real important to keep this island happy, for it has a lot of things left in its womb. That canister was one of them. It had originally belonged to the Navy. Back in the '20s, a Navy officer stationed on the island took to exploring it. He came to this very cave and found a strange glowing liquid growing on the rocks down here. He also found these."

The flashlight's beam moved beyond Bielagus to the cave's wall behind him. It illuminated a rudimentary painting that showed a group of squat humanoids dancing around a fire. The fire was circular and looked like a ring of lit candles. In the middle of it stood a gigantic figure. Its head was vaguely like a cephalopod's, while its torso and legs were hairy like a mammal's. The picture was revolting.

"The Navy man told his superiors, but they questioned his sanity. They kept him on limited duty until he was scheduled to be transferred to Portsmouth, but before he went, he opened one of the canisters that housed the liquid that he found here. It spread throughout the base, and eventually the National Guard had to come in and clean out the place. They killed everyone on the island and told the Navy to reman it before anyone got suspicious.

"No one stayed on the base for long, and after Korea they closed it down. Some places are just too old for the average human's intelligence. Me and Harold can take it though, for we know what really lives underneath this island."

The flashlight again rose to illuminate the sickening creature at the center of the painting. Bielagus's heart sank under the weight of Geoff's suggestion. He heard the hammer pull back.

"That's enough for now. Harold's going to come over there and light one of those wires in your lap. Don't try anything funny. This is really for the best."

Harold shuffled towards Bielagus. He dropped the flashlight next to Bielagus's right leg. As he bent down to pick up the candle in the middle, Bielagus grabbed the flashlight and hit Harold in

his temple. The old man fell down hard with the candle facing his shirt. The flame spread quickly and within seconds the flame was burning away Harold's chest.

Geoff had opened fire after Bielagus's first move. The bullets were erratic and bounced off the cave's many rocks. One of them ricocheted and hit Geoff in his hand. He let out a low bark of pain and dropped the weapon. Bielagus rushed Geoff with Harold's flashlight in his hand. He put the beam right in Geoff's face, thus obscuring the man's vision. Bielagus grabbed the dropped weapon and pointed it at Geoff's head.

"Bullets seem to hurt you. In zombie movies it's always a head shot that does them in. Let's see if Hollywood got it right for once." Bielagus unloaded the revolver's remaining bullets into Geoff's head. Of the three shots, only one hit the old man point-blank. A small, dark, and thick pool of blood collected beneath the man's head. The rotting smell that Bielagus had first sensed back at the cottage grew stronger, plus now it was joined by the smell of burning flesh. Harold was still on fire when Bielagus went back to the boat.

***

"That's quite some tale, Mr. Bielagus. Did the boatman pick you up the next morning?"

"Yeah. I told him nothing, even though he kept asking about the bag."

"I never liked nosey people. Gossips are no good either. I must say that you acquitted yourself quite well. Because of that I've decided to increase your payment by another thousand. Your check is in the mail as we speak."

"Thanks. What are you going to do about the cottage now?"

"Why burn it down of course. The state's historical preservation society will be furious, but I'll hire a man who'll make all the traces back to me disappear. Then I'll act in front of the cameras with contrived surprise. That'll be it basically. My wife has decided to rescind the divorce request. We're making a go of it again, so I now my collection can return back to where it belongs."

Orndorff put his feet on his desk and lit a cigar. He smiled to himself before offering Bielagus a nip from his whiskey bottle. Bielagus held up his hand.

"Between you and me, you need a new hobby."

With that Bielagus left the office hoping to never see Orndorff and his smug, fat face again.

The End.

Case #75444

Ben Welton

Benjamin Welton is a freelance journalist, critic, and essayist who occasionally dabbles in short fiction and poetry. His work has appeared in **The Atlantic**, **The Airship Daily**, **Crime Magazine**, **Ravenous Monster**, **Schlock!**, **Out of the Gutter**, and **Thuglit**. He writes weekly columns and reviews for **InYourSpeakers** and **Doommantia**, plus he is currently working on a novel. His first book - ***Hands Dabbled in Blood*** - is currently available as an ebook on Amazon, iTunes, and Barnes & Noble.

Benjamin's personal blog: http://literarytrebuchet.blogspot.com/

Shacked Up

Daniel Flaherty

Physician: Dr. Peterson
8268-WCT29

THERE WAS A SHACK IN JERRY BOYER'S backyard that he had been constructing himself. It was almost completed, all it needed now was a door. One afternoon, Jerry grabbed a thermos of lemonade and took it out to the shack to privately gloat over his handiwork. He sat down on the concrete floor, sipped lemonade and pictured what tools he would lean where and how the wall he was leaning against would be a great place to store the toolbox.

When Jerry woke up, it was dark. He sat up and stretched. It was getting chilly and he guessed that he should go back to the house.

Moaning a little from the stiffness caused by falling asleep in such a weird position, Jerry picked up the thermos. He took a few steps toward the doorway and stopped. It wasn't obvious right away in the dark, but once he saw it there was no ignoring it: a large spider had built its web all across the threshold.

The sudden sight of the spider sent snapping spots of shock in Jerry's brain and he jumped back. He would have ran into the rear wall of the shack, but thought: what if there's another spider hanging from that back wall? Jerry stood completely still, afraid of startling something into movement. He tried to detect if there was anything on him, and at first he thought there was, tapping forward gingerly on his neck, and his arm shot into action to slap a hand over the movement. He stood still again, keeping his hand pressed hard against his neck, ensuring that nothing could remain alive under that crushing pressure. To make sure that it was dead, Jerry slid his hand across the skin of his neck so the spider would not only be crushed, but smeared. Slowly he pulled his hand away, and then bracing himself brought his hand into view and stared at it.

It was wet, but not with the discolored viscera of spider innards, but plain, clear liquid. Sweat.

He lifted his head so he could look up at the spider in the doorway and make sure it was real and not a figment of his imagination. He couldn't see the web in the minimal light, but there was no mistaking the identification of that huge blob that floated before him.

Getting a visual on the spider and knowing that it wasn't going to move at him, Jerry was able to observe the spider with a kind of repulsed fascination. He could see it suspended there waiting for some prey to come in contact with its web. Jerry felt a breeze drift in from outside and watched the spider float forward and back again.

Jerry's leg muscles were starting to cramp due to their flexed tension and the stiff way he was standing. He had to sit down; he couldn't stay standing.

He looked at the spot he had been resting against earlier, tried to see through the darkness if there was anything there or the surrounding wall and ceiling. It was too dark. Still, the urge to rest was too great and he turned tentatively and eased himself down, his hands bunched into fists and held against his chest in anticipation.

He wished he had a blanket, something to keep out the cold. He imagined a blanket, a special one that was soft inside and emitted a radiation that kept spiders away. He imagined himself cocooned inside this blanket, while outside it was bitter cold and crawling with spiders. After a while, Jerry fell asleep.

He woke up when the sun was up, and it was such a pleasant day that he could image for a while that it had just been some kind of dream. Jerry lifted his head from the bench and looked at the threshold. There it was, still there and in the bright reality of daylight there was no denying its fact.

Jerry stood up and moved as close as he dared to the spider to get a better look at it. The spider had built the web from the outside so that Jerry was looking at its underbelly. Its abdomen was a light brown and he could see the gill-like segmented grooves that would allow it flexibility. Was it an optical illusion or could Jerry actually see its abdomen pulse with girth?

Jerry leaned down and picked up his thermos. Establishing a firm grip, he pulled his arm back and allowed a moment to aim. Hit it dead on, he told himself, and send it traveling along with the momentum of the thermos. Send it way out there in the woods and maybe the thermos will land on top of it on impact to ensure its demise.

Jerry threw the thermos. It smashed through the web, breaking a waving gap in the web and crashed out among the leaves, about fifteen yards out.

At first, Jerry didn't see the spider. He saw that where the spider had been, there was now a gaping hole left by the thermos. Jerry felt a moment of championed relief, but that didn't last long because then he spotted the spider scurrying upwards towards the thresholds upper frame. Once there, it searched around for a bit like a dog looking for a place to lie, and then dropped down, its legs splayed out to create a safety drag. These legs began scrambling and clutching about when they came in contact with some remaining threads and Jerry had to watch as the spider began reconstructing its web.

While the spider worked, Jerry pulled his shoes off and lifted them, one in each hand. He was going to take care of this once and for all. He threw the first shoe, giving it a sideways hurl to take out a larger stretch of the web. The spider had been pulling itself back up to the upper sill when Jerry had made the toss, but his shoe had still taken out a hefty chunk of the web, almost severing it in half. The spider seemed to sense it was under attack and stayed in place on the sill and this was fine for Jerry. He shifted his remaining shoe over to his right hand and crept up closer to the threshold, eyes bulging and his tongue poking from the corner of his mouth. Then he swiped at the spider, making sure he got close enough to make contact, and he heard the "thunk" sound when the toe of the shoe scraped against the sill. And after the shoe had made its path, the spider was gone.

Jerry stared at the spot where the spider had been, wide eyed and a dopey grin on his face, almost not believing that the nightmare was over. Finally, he gave a cheer and hopped up and down.

He was holding the shoe still and it was only the peripheral glimpse of movement that made him look down at the shoe to see that the spider was crawling over the ridge of the toe and making for his hand. Jerry made a deep gasp and flung the shoe away, and it took out more of the web before falling right outside the shack.

Jerry stood there watching the shoe to see if the spider would make an appearance, and it did. It crawled over the dirt and fallen vegetation, making a busy path for the shack's threshold.

Go now, Jerry told himself. I can leave and go back home now. Jerry reached out to tear away the remains of the web that still hung in the way. His hand hovered hesitantly before the strands and Jerry felt his arm turn hard in resistance.

Do it, just tear it away with your hand or run through it! The spider isn't there yet, just run through!

Jerry made himself reach out further and his fingertips actually touched the web. As soon as he came in contact with it, when he felt its fluffy, yet rough stickiness, a texture he thought he could

actually hear, Jerry pulled his hand away and jumped back. He couldn't touch that! He couldn't run through that!

And already he saw the spider scrambling up the side of the threshold and he knew it was too late.

***

Jerry knew that he was in trouble. The spider had rebuilt its web, strong and big as ever. It even had some kind of insect trapped in it. The spider was clutching itself over its prey and feeding on it, getting even bigger and fatter as a result.

Lower down on the web was Jerry's shirt, hovering and trapped there: the result of another one of his attempts to knock out the spider and destroy its web.

It was a hot out and Jerry hadn't had anything to drink in two days. Out there, seen past through the veil of webbing was the thermos of lemonade. Why couldn't he go out there and get that thermos and ease his thirst? Why couldn't he leave his shack, his "sanctuary" and go home?

The spider hovered there before him, its body twitching as it sucked out the trapped insect's fluids. Jerry's focus repeatedly went from the thermos to the spider and back to the thermos. He had his arms pressed tight against his ribs; his fists balled up next to his chin. "Eee!" he squealed, his eyes bulging. He looked more like a six-year-old girl who had been told she was getting a pony for her birthday, rather than a grown man held prisoner by an arachnid and suffering from dehydration.

What kind of fucked up flaw in human evolution *was* this?

***

"Jerry? *Jerry?*"

Who was that? Jerry knew that voice. It was Rudy Coates from down the street. Rudy was a good friend and had helped Jerry with some of the heavier work in the shack's construction.

"Oh, Christ! Jerry! How did--"

Jerry opened his eyes. There was nobody there. He was alone in the shack. Why had he heard Rudy's voice? Had he been dreaming? It had seemed so real though, like his friend had actually been there standing over him.

Jerry sat up. He was feeling disconcerted right now, but that was no surprise. Being without food or drink had caused a mental deterioration that had left him far from feeling normal.

There was a sound coming from a distance outside and it was getting closer.

Jerry got to his feet and stood by the threshold, looking out through the doorway. It was the sounds of approaching feet coming from the side of his house. Some kind of animal? No…no, those footfalls—and with the now unmistakable addition of voices, Jerry knew: *people.*

Dehydration had scorched Jerry's throat these last few days, so the thought of using his voice should have seemed unbearable. Yet when he yelled, it was without discomfort and his yell was loud and true.

"HEY! Over here! I'm out here! Help!" The tonnage of his voice boomed with strength, and the birds took flight all at once from the trees, the collective beat of their wings like someone flapping a gigantic sheet. "Help!"

And then the approaching people came into view and the dream must have been a premonition because one of the men was Rudy.

"Hey! Rudy! Over here, man! I'm here!"

***

Rudy had called the police and when they arrived, he took them out to the shack where he had found Jerry.

One of the officers looked in the shack and quickly pulled his head back out.

"Christ, Jesus!" he said, covering his mouth and nose. Holding his breath, he stuck his head back in and took a look at the half-decayed corpse that lay oozing away on the floor. Satisfied that the deceased was truly dead he stepped back and removed his hand.

"Yeah, that guy's dead alright." He looked at Rudy. "How long ago was it since you saw him last?"

"About two weeks. We usually get together two, three times a week, and at least on weekends, but I hadn't heard from him and he wasn't answering his phone calls. Finally, I came out to check up on him and when he didn't answer his door, I went out back to check, and--"

Rudy shut up. He ran a hand through his hair which was stringy with sweat. The two police officers watched him closely. He was pale looking and they were wondering if he was going to pass out on them.

One of the officers turned his head and then hunched down to look at a shoe that was lying on the ground. He looked up and moved his gaze around to see if there was another shoe around. Yes, there was just a couple of feet from where his partner and Rudy were talking.

"Hey, Mike," the officer said and nodded his head when his partner looked at him. "This shoe here and that one next to you. Did you notice if the deceased was barefoot?"

Mike hadn't noticed. The corpse had been such a mess that he had only made note on the state of the body. And since he was now alert for any more possible discarded clothing items, he saw the shirt that was half in and half out of the shack. Mike took another deep breath, prepared himself, and then stuck his head back in the shack for another look at the body. No shirt, and no shoes.

When he pulled his head back out, his partner was looking at him.

"What do you think?" he asked.

Mike didn't know what to think. There weren't any signs of violence, but it was obvious that this hadn't been a normal death, that something odd had happened.

***

There had been people around, a bunch of them, and Jerry thought they would help him. But then they had all gone away. Things were slipping from his mind. He was forgetting. He remembered that one of the people was familiar to him somehow and that once he had known that man's name. But now when he tried to think of what that name could have been, he came up blank.

And the *why* of things, he was forgetting those too. Like, there had been something in the doorway, something bad that had been keeping him here. Whatever that thing had been, it was gone now and Jerry should have been able to leave. But every time he got close to the threshold his skin would start tickling and he would get a feeling of something tangling itself in his hair.

Jerry clutched the sides of his head and let out a howl of frustration. In response, a dog began barking furiously. Jerry focused his eyes in the dark and saw the dog out there straining against the edge of a rope. The dog was making short lunges like it was trying to get at Jerry. He could see the dog's eyes trained on him as it kept barking.

The back porch light to Jerry's house suddenly snapped on and the back door was flung open. Silhouetted in the light, Jerry saw a man in shorts and he felt new hope.

"Hey! Out here! Help me!"

"Shut up!" the man yelled.

"Help me, *please*!"

"Goddammit! I said shut up!"

The dog kept barking.

"Wookie, come here!"

The dog stopped it barking and looked at the man.

"Come!"

The dog looked once more out at Jerry and then, surrendering, trotted over to the man.

"Come here," the man said, grabbing the dog by the collar and undoing its leash. "Get in there! Stupid mutt."

"Wait! Wait!" Jerry wailed as he watched the man return back in the house and shut the door behind him. The porch light switched off and again there was darkness.

Jerry dropped his arm. Trapped. *Trapped*.

The End.

Case #46214

Daniel Flaherty

Daniel Flaherty lives in Portland, Oregon where he fixes light rail vehicles for the city's public transportation system. He also likes to write and his stories have appeared in <u>Down in the Dirt</u> and <u>Dark Eclipse</u> magazines.

Coated in Canvas

James Park

Physician: Dr. Peterson
8268-WCT29

Each drop expanded into circles, growing slowly, rippling across the water until they popped. Then there was nothing. All was still until the faucet released another drop; a faint pitter-patter resonated as it hit the surface. Her arms glistened. Soapy water stirred throughout the tub. The world was motionless as she closed her eyes. Steam rose, hovering in suspension as if an inferno had roared its flames, heating the tub, erupting like fire within the young woman's heart. The moment lingered for what seemed like hours, but vanished with the bat of an eyelash. Time held no barriers as she soaked her tired limbs to recover from a long day's work. She withdrew arousal from the daily routine, absorbing his attention, pulling him in like a vulture, forcing his eyes to trace every curve of her petite body. She kicked her legs, sending light ripples through the water. A soft pitter-patter echoed as another drop fell from the faucet.

She liked to give Jake a show, elevating her soapy leg as water dripped down the thigh, arms in V-formation, her upper body extending past the surface. Eye contact was avoided. Jake wasn't to know that she'd caught him peeping. Life would continue as normal if the platonic relationship wasn't tampered with. Besides, he was masked behind the canvas coating of a hideous face. She never really saw him—just eyes peeping through the frame, visible from every corner of the room yet shielded by her lack of recognition. Angela yawned as she rested her head against the white tiled wall, long strands of golden hair dangling over her bare shoulders. She was tired. There wouldn't be much of a show today, just a glance at her nakedness.

There hadn't always been an attraction between the two, at least not on Angela's part. Her attraction for Jake didn't ripen until their senior year of high school, when his adolescent acne cleared, leaving behind smooth skin to accentuate his well-chiseled features.

The days of teenage lust, gossip in the hallways, and the sight of Jake in his wrestling singlet eventually came to an end. The sweat and tears were gone. Images of Jake pinning opponents against the mat faded faster than she anticipated. The glory was over. She retired her pompoms.

Their young adult lives arrived, presenting different daily routines, altered social styles, and, in an attempt to break free from beneath their parent's wings, new living arrangements. Facing the cold contour of the world went hand-in-hand with the newfound freedom. Life was satisfying, but hard. They'd agreed to co-rent a Victorian-styled townhouse—a cozy little abode resting in a decent neighborhood surrounded by coffee houses and a quaint little park where children played, squirrels collected nuts, and birds swooped with open wings. The arrangement had been strictly for the sake of economics. It kept them away from the low rent high-rises and other defiled buildings that deface the outskirts of town. And by sharing the rent, neither of them was forced to shatter their piggy bank.

Dreams of breaking past the barrier of friendship danced through Angela's mind as bubbles floated atop soapy water. A thick fog coated the mirror as she took yet another glance, checking, making sure the eyes hadn't wandered. She thought about him often, and wondered if they had a future, but she'd never mustered the courage to make an advance. She came close on the day they moved in. At first, just the thought of spending night after night under the same roof as Jake aroused deep emotions. It became painful. Lust pulled at her gut when they left the suburbs—such a tiresome day. Hours were consumed by tedious work. Rubbish lined the walls, the spiral staircase, hiding in every closet. They'd found empty beer cans, marijuana pipes, even an old gym sock balled up and abandoned in the corner of a room that stank of mildew. Decayed flowers rested atop the windowsills marked by dry leaves that crumbled at the touch. The painting was found in the bathroom, where it remains, suspended atop pale walls; it stares over the old-fashioned tub. There's no doubt that the artist slaved over the piece, having captured a true essence of realism with every brushstroke. Colors swoon in and out of each other, fading toward a serene darkness that eases into the canvas corners. Beauty was sacrificed for the harsh reality of truth.

"It's an eyesore," Angela complained, squinting in disgust at the image of an aged man in his upper-seventies with liver spots discoloring his cheeks. He'd been painted with all the dignity that a man of age can receive, suited in a smoking jacket, a gleaming maze scarf wrapped around his neck. But the teeth were moldy and the eyes, of course, were missing. Two dark holes were carved where the eyes had been painted, making it possible for anyone to peep from the bedroom closet and catch a glance at whoever was using the tub.

"We're leaving it right where it is," Jake insisted, arms outstretched as his cheeks flushed. At first Angela didn't understand the reasoning for his demand. She pleaded, begging him to remove the revolting portrait, but his say was final, and the monstrosity remained.

Hardly a week passed before Angela pieced the puzzle together, making it even harder to cloak her attraction. When she first noticed the holes in the painting—and the peeping eyes that watched from the bedroom closet—it felt like butterflies were flapping their wings inside her stomach. She kept silent, granting the eyes the privilege of spying on her, and she gained spine-curdling arousal from every bath that followed.

She twisted her smooth neck just to grasp a peek at the wandering eyes, then sank back into the tub as they watched, inspecting her figure. Water swept over her soft skin as bubbles rippled their way toward the surface. Angela felt the urge growing, fluttering in her stomach. She'd fought it for weeks, keeping the dirty little secret to herself, but she couldn't submerge the enthrallment. It felt like demons had been conjured by Jake's interest in her body, and she wanted the demons to have their way.

Drops of water trickled from the faucet, forming rings atop the surface, growing until they broke into nothing. A soft pitter-patter echoed above the drain.

Other than that, silence prevailed.

They'd been friends since the sixth grade and neither of them wanted to jeopardize what they had, but the attraction and the yearning grew. Its intensity drifted through the air like steam rising from the tub. She was afraid. *What if unraveling the scenario humiliated Jake? What if he could no longer face me?*

She kicked her legs—toes pointed, feet curved—while arching her back, breasts resting above the water. She glanced at the picture. The eyes watched, glued to every insignificant move she made. Slowly, as her pulse accelerated, Angela rose from the tub, facing a hideous man with beautiful blue eyes. She stretched, water dripping from her body, pitter-pattering against the surface, intensity building with every drop, every beat. Streaks of water ran past her belly as she wondered what would happen. *What if I confront him?* The yearning tickled her insides, growing until her entire body shivered. *Enough's enough,* she thought, crossing the room and passing through the door.

"Oh, Jake? Yoo-hoo, Jake?" she called as her feet skipped across the floor. His door was ajar. Faint rays of setting sunlight streamed from the crack, spilling into the hallway. She pushed the door open and it creaked, commencing a chain reaction that flowed through the townhouse. Floorboards echoed, walls resonated, and mice scurried through gaps in the walls as the house settled. Jake was still, sprawled across the bed, head tilted at an unusual angle. A faint cry from outside slipped through the window, gliding over the bed. Children laughed. Children screamed.

Jake was silent. Motionless.

"Jake?" The beat of her heart quickened. The butterflies in her stomach took off in all directions, poking at her belly as a soft breeze seeped from the open window and swept through the room, sending a chill across her nakedness. Outside, leaves crackled beneath tiny feet. Children ran, playing their game of hide and go seek. Angela leapt, landing atop Jake's outstretched body. "Gotcha!" she squealed before her smile melted away.

Her clean white calves turned dark purple as a thick fluid seeped up her thigh, slowly coating the flesh and eventually forming a thick puddle between her legs. A cloud passed before the sun, casting a dim shadow over the Victorian-styled townhouse. Angela sat atop the moist sheets, surrounded by darkness, confounded, unable to scream as the closet door opened. The hinges creaked but Angela heard nothing. She stared over the body. A deep incision roamed across Jake's throat, stretching from cheek to cheek, ending just below the ears. He was cold, pulse still, as if the body hadn't stirred for some time.

Angela froze, unable to comprehend.

Fingertips tickled her back. Leather gloves assumed a position on her motionless shoulders, sending a chill down her spine that caused hairs to stand on end. A gust of warm breath blew past he ear, ensuing goosebumps atop her arms. Gloved fingers ran through long strands of wet golden hair. A car horn honked. The laughter of children danced through the air. "Dinner time," a mother called. Angela could hear the children scurrying from the park as a leather glove stroked her curves. The sun was just beginning to set. Couples roamed in and out of nearby coffee houses. The stench of ground beans and cigarette smoke drifted through the air, past the curtains, and spread throughout the room. He cupped her chin between leathery fingers, molding both palms around the curves of her delicate face, twisting the head until they faced each other. She stared deep into his blue eyes. They were similar to Jake's but more beautiful with thousands of shades sweeping through the ocean-like balls. Time stood still as she studied every feature of the face. She'd seen him before. It was a familiar mug that she couldn't quite place a name with. Their mouths opened as he leaned in, their soft lips parting to the lash of his tongue. Reality was lost. Time continued to pass. Their mouths formed a vortex as the tongues wrestled one another, lashing back and forth. The setting sun cast an iridescent glow across her pallid flesh. He broke away from the kiss and held her between open palms, a hand on either cheek.

* *** *

Hours strolled away, vanishing before the men in white broke down the front door and rushed up the spiral staircase. Their feet hardly grazed the floor. They found her naked, hiding in the corner of the adjacent bedroom, curled into a ball. A trail of blood ran from her body, roaming through the hallway and ending on Jake's bed. She was cold, shivering as they lifted her up. Soaked in blood, tears streaming from child-like eyes, her trembling lips parted to murmur, "J-J-Jake never saw me n-n-aked."

She fell silent.

A brief hospital stay followed the erogenous display of affection. Not a single IV pierced her tender flesh. No *physical* damage had occurred. They transferred her during the wee hours of the morning, as the spring sun rose above budding trees. The daylight was overwhelming, scorching the earth with ultraviolet rays as the men in white wrapped Angela in canvas clothing, arms folded atop one another, the sleeves bound tightly behind her back. They escorted the fearful mind into the melancholy walls of a nearby facility. Angela was like a prisoner, dragged beneath pale lights that once possessed a bright neon glow. Insects hovered around the source, buzzing. They were everywhere, coating walls with open wings and microscopic legs. The men in white gripped the canvas coated arms as they pulled Angela toward a diminutive room with a musty cot, a screen across the window, and a slot in the door for trays of food to slide in and out.

She never touches the slop.

Ever since, she sits in the corner and shakes, twitches, nervous convulsions ruling her world. They feed her with a needle. Days come and go as her condition shifts, slightly improving until nightmares, hallucinations, and tainted reminiscence cause her mentality to plummet. She often says, "The walls are closing in," before hiding her face in canvas-coated arms. She tells doctors to stay away from paintings. For reasons the psychiatrists can't comprehend, she refuses to bathe. Her odor grows as days pass.

Angela awaits her last. It's coming soon.

The End.

Case #25609

James Park

James Park lives in Columbus, Ohio with his gorgeous and delightfully articulate wife Ngouanephone. His hobbies include watching independent pro wrestling, collecting rare horror movies, and attending heavy metal shows. He enjoys writing and has been featured in a number of genre fiction publications, including Dark Moon Digest, Ghostlight Magazine, and Cemetery Moon.

New work is scheduled to appear in upcoming issues of Infernal Ink Magazine, Night to Dawn Magazine, and Massacre Magazine. He has contributed horror stories to several upcoming anthologies, including The New Whakazoid Circus, Lost in the Witching Hour, and Moon Shadows, and will have a piece of well-crafted smut published in the Apologues' of Erotica anthology.

CLAYTON HILL SANITARIUM

Dark Verse

Physician: Dr. Salam
7128-DV758JJ

James Michael Shoberg
Alex Bardy
R. Bremner

Doug never liked his grandma's house. It had a surly soul,
Which pumped out of its hellish heart—the furnace, "Old King Coal."
"That's what your grandpa called it, dear, when he was with us still.
He'd say, 'This is his castle, and we're guests, so mind his will.'"
Yes, 'willful,' that describes our metal monarch well, you know.
For when he means to have his way, he'll make such noise below!
We bought this place while in our youth—the home, already old.
That furnace was original, or, so the owner told:
'Sure it's a cranky, clanky brute, but if you keep him full,
You'll find no newer model to be as reliable!'
Throughout the years, the owner's words were proven to be fact.
We'd keep him full; he'd keep us warm—a fair, unspoken pact."
Her story didn't comfort Doug, who'd run the cellar stairs,
Convinced "King Coal" would reach with pipes and catch him unawares.
But Doug, who loved his grandma, and did everything she asked,
Would brave the basement nonetheless, whenever he was tasked.
One day his parents dropped him off. They had a date to dine.
"Don't leave me here till morning!" They responded, "You'll be fine."
Doug spent a pleasant evening which in time put him at ease.
Though soon, that calm was spoiled by the simplest of pleas.
"Doug, do Grandma a kindness, and feed 'Old King Coal' some lumps.
I'm rather sore this evening, and he's due to start his thumps."
"Oh Grandma, do I—" "Douglas, I know he can seem a fright, But we need heat, and truth be told, he likes to run at night.
Just think yourself a soldier, who's been called to serve the king. It shouldn't take a moment, Doug, to do this tiny thing."
So Doug, who loved his grandma, and did everything she asked,
Proceeded down the creaky steps, his terror poorly masked.
And that's when the idea came to simply stop and wait.
"I'll stand here for the time it takes, and she'll assume he ate." However, guilt had surfaced, shortly after he

returned,When Grandma tucked him into bed, and gave the
kiss he'd "earned."
Doug spent long, restless hours, burdened by the trick he played.
And thought, as pipes began to moan, "Go fix the mess you made!"
He tiptoed through a quiet house, to face his devil's door.
Before he knew, his slippered feet were on the cellar floor.
In Doug's imagination he heard, "Kneel before me, son!
And beg 'King Coal's' forgiveness for the wrong which you have
done!"
Doug took hold of the shovel leaning on the nearby bin,
Believing just a scoop or two would rid him of his sin.
But when he glanced into the shoot, he saw the lumps were few.
"It doesn't look like there's enough to make a scoop or two!" He
leaned as far as possible to stretch the shovel out. And when he
lost his balance, he fell with a stifled shout.
"I hope that Grandma's still asleep," the boy thought, black with
dust.
That's when the sound of moaning was replaced by cracking rust.
Doug raised his head up from the bin, and with no great surprise,
He saw what he had always known take place before his eyes.
"King Coal" was pulling himself free. He wanted to be fed.
His pipes were raised like "tin-tacles," above his angry head.
A legless base slid screeching as it crossed the cold concrete.
Doug jumped out of the filthy box and tangled up his feet.
Now frozen—one foot bare—he stared into a searing hole. A
fearsome, flaming, metal maw, that spoke but one word—
"COAL."
Doug's skin and his pajamas were both soiled as could be.
"And in whatever eyes he has, he sees a meal in me!"
I won't describe what took place next—the lesson late to learn.
Just know, within a furnace, little liars quickly burn.
The screaming woke his grandma who observed a quiet scene,
Though glimpsed a telling object from which all she now could
glean.
Before "the King," a single, dirty slipper caught her sight.
Then Grandma said, "I warned you, Doug: 'He likes to run at
night.'
I'll tell the truth—you 'disappeared'—although, it won't assuage.
But Grandma can't afford another furnace at her age."

Case #51847

James Michael Shoberg

JAMES MICHAEL SHOBERG has many years of diverse experience in theatre. He is an award-winning actor and playwright, as well as a designer and director. His writing credits include numerous fringe plays and collections of both monologues and poems. James is also the Co-Executive Producer/Artistic Director/Resident Playwright of The Rage of the Stage Players fringe theatre company in Pittsburgh, Pennsylvania, now entering its thirteenth season. In 2011, he acquired the permission of the filmmakers known as The Butcher Brothers, and Lionsgate Films, to write, produce, and direct a world-premiere stage adaptation of their award-winning independent horror film, The Hamiltons, for The Rage of the Stage Players. In October 2013, they premiered his latest play, a steampunk stage adaptation of Oscar Wilde's, The Picture of Dorian Gray. James' unique brand of twisted theatre has already attracted attention both nationally and internationally, and he is always seeking new venues for future productions of his work. His most recent side project is a currently untitled book of horror poetry for young adults.

CLAYTON HILL SANITARIUM

Wisps of cloud pass across a pale-lit moon. Leaves

rustle, a-spinning and a-twirling, Flirting

With the edge of the pavement.

A black raven squawks nearby,

It flies up and away,

Squawking and cawing,

Ascending

Into a damp, wet-kissed morning.

A car screeches to a halt on the corner.

Everything fades to black.

And all because you watched the bird, And

dared to dance

With a pale-lit moon in a wet morning sky..

Case #96643

Alex Bardy

Alex Bardy lives in a very dark place, below a small dank stairwell, beneath a dark step, under a speck of dirt, tucked away in a cold, dark emptiness, somewhere on the fringes of the charming historical City of York, in the North Yorkshire area of the UK. He also writes as DenizenOfTheUniverse under his Twitter moniker: @mangozoid. He is a contributor, reviewer, and word-lender to the British Fantasy Society (BFS - www.britishfantasysociety.co.uk), and an active member on the board of the British Science Fiction Association (BSFA - www.bsfa.co.uk), mailnly responsible for the layout and design of their exclusive member publications, with an occasional foray into writing fiction, poetry, features, and interviewing.

That wicked hobgoblin and its demonic companion plot
their merciless wickedness to do me
I know, I can feel their devilish presence though
see them or hear them I cannot I go through this
rigamarole every night Once I drift off to
slumber they come to purloin my pleasant hours
of dreams I can smell them but never can see
them as they plot plot plot my demise
and ruin my pure sleep with their hijinks

Case #14554

R. Bremner

R. Bremner has been writing stories, nonfiction essays, and poetry for forty years.

In the past six years, he has suffered a fractured shoulder, a near-fatal kidney infection, a stroke in 2010 that still affects the right side of his face, a liver transplant in 2011, followed by a broken hip in 2012, but he keeps on writing, by the grace of God! He has worked as a cab driver, a UPS truck unloader, a security guard, a computer programmer, and a bank vice-president, and he has published in International Poetry Review, Inclement, Turbulence, Title Waves, the Passaic Review, Poets Online, Every Writer's Resource, Ancient Paths, and the Mensa Bulletin, among others. Among his ebooks are *Stories of Love and Hate, Poems for the Narrow, Dog Stories, Nightmares: the Halloween Edition (poems of sheer terror), You are once again the stranger, Murder in Glen Ridge,* and *Lovers' Suite, 37 Poems of Passion.* All are available on Amazon, Barnes and Noble, Itunes, Sony, Kobo and Diesel. He lives in Glen Ridge, NJ, USA with his lovely wife, a sociology professor, their brilliant son, and their excitable puppy Ariel (named for the Sylvia Plath poem).

On the
Record

A Moment With Shaun Hutson

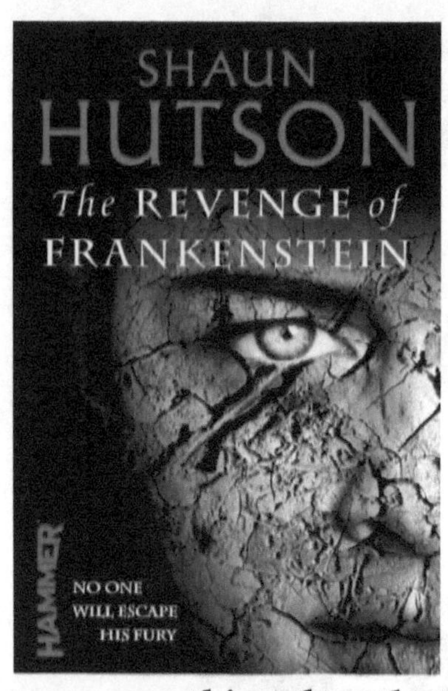

Interview by Andy Squires.

Thanks very much for taking the time to speak to us. First up, the nicknames. *Emperor of Excess, Godfather of Gore, Shakespeare of Gore.* You've collected quite a few monikers over your career, is there one that you're particularly proud of?

I like all of them to be honest. I've picked up some names I'm not so proud of too but I figure that as long as someone remembers me as something then that's fine. Also, after spilling so much blood in print over the years I'd be a bit of a twat to object to those nicknames. ..As I said, it's better to be remembered for something.

Growing up you were a big fan of the *Hammer* movies. Are there any titles in particular that stuck with you, and have those early experiences influenced your writing to this point?

Hammer films always had a touch of class (not that I'd attempt to suggest my writing was classy!) but it was their integrity and style that always impressed me. The visual style and everything about the early ones (up to about 1966) was superb and I think it was just the whole Gothic feel that made such an impression on me as a youngster. My novels were always contemporary but I always felt they had a kind of Gothic feel to them no matter what they were about and Hammer are to thank for that. As for individual titles, I would say BRIDES OF DRACULA, PLAGUE OF THE ZOMBIES and THE CURSE OF FRANKENSTEIN have been the films that made the deepest impression on me.

You also got to write a novelisation of *The Revenge of Frankenstein*. That must have been a great experience, how did writing that differ to the process of creating your own books?

Doing that novelization was great. I felt very privileged. It was a real treat to do something for/with Hammer but also it gave me the chance to add little touches but without ever deviating from the original ideas. Obviously, with an original novel it's all your own work as it were but with a novelization all the basics are there for you, it's just a matter of fleshing things out and trying to enhance what's already there. I loved it and it's a pity they aren't doing any more.

What do you think about the state of the horror genre today, are you a fan of the books/films that are being written/ made now?

What horror genre? Have we still got one? The horror section in most bookshops (if there is a horror section which is rare) consists of Stephen King, Dean Koontz, a few copies of some newer books and shelves of sci-fi or comics. The publishing business has ensured that horror has been more or less killed off. The films that are being made now are mostly shite. Just continuations of the PARANORMAL ACTIVITY franchise or more "found footage" films. Either that or it's all remakes of earlier films (The Texas Chainsaw Massacre, Friday the 13th etc. etc.). There's no imagination and no attempts to take a chance on anything new. The horror genre is stagnant, despite readers' desires for more horror books. Books like TWILIGHT have destroyed it with their sanitisation of traditional horror.

In your early career you would often switch between genres, writing whatever your publishers were asking for. As well as horror, you have written westerns, war stories and books about UFOs. Did you find it tough to switch between styles and topics?

Not at all. If someone is professional enough then they should find it no problem to work in different genres. You don't have to change styles after all, just settings and dialogue! I loved changing genres too, it was fun and it let me explore subjects I wouldn't have done normally in the horror genre. I wrote

whatever publishers wanted and if I was getting paid for it I couldn't care less which genre I was working in.

Do you think that method of 'writing to order' still happens these days?

I wouldn't know to be honest. Publishing has changed too much in the last ten or fifteen years. There are no characters in it anymore, no "showmanship" for want of a better word. When I started there were individual publishers who were known for different subjects and people within the business who were well known for their expertise but now it's just a collection of faceless conglomerates. The same goes for the authors too. No characters, no personalities. With so many publishers only interested in "celebrity" books there's no sign of that changing either.

You have a pretty phenomenal work ethic; you've had over 60 books published under both your name and pseudonyms, and I believe you once wrote a 45,000 word story in five days. What keeps you writing?

What kept me writing in those days was a love of what I was doing. Being young and full of enthusiasm I really cared about sharing ideas and stories with people and publishers were only too happy to support that. If the money was right I'd probably produce a 45,000 word story in five days even now! Motivation changes as you get older (well it did for me anyway). Back then, a writer came up with an idea and just wrote it and if a publisher liked it that was fine but now everything is different. The big names do what they want to do and everyone else jumps through hoops.

In recent years, due to the internet, there has been an explosion of self-publishing options available to new and existing writers. What are your thoughts on the way the publishing industry is heading?

Self-publishing is one of the worst things ever to happen to the book business if you want an honest opinion. It means there is no "quality control" (although looking at some of the shit that publishers churn out that term is probably redundant anyway!).

Anyone with an idea and a printer suddenly thinks they're a writer and that isn't how it works. It's the same with all the blogs on different sites. Writing a blog doesn't make you an author, sorry! As for the way the publishing industry is heading... er...I'm probably the wrong person to ask. There'll always be a publishing industry that's for sure but what form it will take is anyone's guess.

You have also written content exclusively for online. Do you like that instant connection that the internet allows you with readers?

It never really mattered to me whether a piece of writing was done for a website, a script or a novel. As long as readers enjoy it that's all that matters. The immediacy of the internet is irrelevant to me, once something is written it's written. Simple as that.

Your book *Slugs* was adapted for film. Would you like to go down that route with any of your other titles?

I'd like to go down that route with EVERY title! If a Hollywood company rang up and said they'd like to film everything I'd ever written I'd be delighted, especially if they were paying a fortune for it! When books are turned into films the end result usually bears little resemblance to the novel anyway so it's just a matter of taking the money and running. Only the big authors get any say in what their novels look like on screen. You have to remember that readers won't think anything less of the novel because the film is shit, readers aren't stupid.

As well as slugs, you've written books about killer foetuses, cults, murderous animals and cannibals amongst many others. Are there any topics that you wouldn't write about?

I wrote about the subjects I wrote about because they were what interested me. I never wrote anything just to create controversy. It just so happened that some of the things I wrote were a little... er...contentious or shocking but I was a horror writer after all. I don't think anyone should ever shy away from writing something just because it might be shocking or controversial, you just have to be careful sometimes about the way you do it. The dictionary

definition of horror is physical revulsion so I must have been doing something right!

What are your plans for the future, any ideas about your next writing project?
My plans for the future right now are...lunch! I finished a book called MONOLITH not long ago but that's it. I have ideas floating around inside my mind most of the time, I always have but what happens to them is another matter. Not much probably... Only time will tell or whichever cliché you prefer.

Thanks again for taking the time to answer our questions. All the best for the future!!

My pleasure...thanks for asking the questions!!

Shaun Hutson is a British novelist, who has written over 60 books, ranging from dark thriller to children's stories. While he has worked in many genres he is best known for his horror novels, titles such as *Slugs*, *Last Rites* and *Nemesis*. Shaun currently lives and works in Milton Keynes and is a lifelong Liverpool FC supporter.

http://www.shaunhutson.com

Can you describe what your workspace is like?

My wife and I recently purchased an 1810 log home in Kentucky, where I finally have room for my own "lair". It's a bit of a cave, there are no windows, but as I spend most of my creative time looking through my mind's eye, that suits me fine. I decorated the place solely with funds from illustration work, so it's very fulfilling to have a space that came from my creative endeavours. Lots of inspiration there, I rather like it!

Do you have a go-to gadget / app or service that you cannot live without?

You know, I know it sounds rather old fashioned, but I've grown very attached to using moleskine books to jot down notes, do sketches and work out ideas. I have one dedicated to Ghost Zero, with the GZ logo embossed on the front. I literally carry the thing everywhere, because I never know when a bit of an idea comes along that I need to "catch". When I first bought the thing, I felt kind of like a "real" writer when I carried it around. Now, it just seems like something that is strange to be without. I'll be picking up one for each of my major projects to use as story bibles.

Do you have a set routine while you work?

Absolutely. In fact, I'm a bit of an evangelist about the importance of scheduling set routines for creative activities. Each evening, I come home from my day job and sit down to dinner with my wife. Promptly at 7:00, I head up to the "lair" for a couple hours of creative time and then have some reading before bed. Writing (or drawing) in two hour "chunks" works best for me. If I work for longer than that without taking a bit of a break, I feel stale and uncreative.

Of course, there are times after a busy day when I don't feel like doing anything but playing video games or watching a movie. When that happens, my wife tells me "Go and try it for fifteen minutes. If you don't feel like it after that, you can quit." It's magic. I go up, fully intending to just knock around for fifteen minutes and then lay off, but I find myself quickly getting into it
and having a really productive evening. This is why I believe the "artistic inspiration" bit of creativity is just hogwash. I often refer to myself as an "idea mechanic" because to really produce a body of creative work, you have to run at it like it's a job. You can't wait for inspiration to strike, or you'll die of old age before you get anything done!

What is the best piece of advice you have ever received?

I actually read something on a blog that really shaped my outlook on writing. The blogger said (and I'm paraphrasing), "Imagine that writing a book is like storming the beach at Normandy. Stuff is flying at you from every direction, but if you let it distract you, you're dead. Your sole job is to get to that damned cliff at the end of the beach. Write like you're running hell-bent for the end of your book. Don't worry about editing it to death, that will come later. Just get the thing done. Hammer it out, because until a book is done, you don't have a book. You have some writing that you're playing with. Get it done."

Do you have a final piece of advice for our readers?

Remember that any time you do something creative and put it out for others to see, it's like pulling your pants down in public. You just feel terribly vulnerable. That is a NORMAL feeling, but you can't let it stop you. Do it anyway, and if it fails horribly, you start working on the next big thing. People don't realize that Mark Twain failed at more things in his life than he succeeded, because success cancels failure. Creating is an odds game. The more you play, the more likely you will win.

About Dave:

Dave Flora grew up on a dairy farm in Kentucky, where a strange combination of rural living, ghost stories and comic books made him the man he is today.

He began drawing superheroes at a young age, and enjoyed creating his own characters and telling stories about them. He never stopped.

Dave has self-published two Ghost Zero comics, *Ghosts with Guns* and *The Vigilante Crypt*, and his 1950's B-movie, sci-fi webcomic, *Doc Monster*, was a finalist in DC Comic's webcomic competition in 2010. He has done numerous illustrations for books, games, and magazines.

Dave has starred in 18 local community theatre productions, was a navy reservist, a Freemason, and once ran over a cow with a tractor. She was fine.

He lives with his wife and cat in an 1810 log cabin. Dave's first novel, *Ghost Zero: Spookshow*, was published in January, and his second novel, *Ghost Zero: The Midnight Society* is due out this spring.

www.daveflora.wordpress.com

If you have any feedback or would like to leave a review, please head over to Amazon and share your thoughts about Sanitarium.

9 798558 735260